A

CONFIDENT

MAN

Discovery Years

PAUL COPELAND

CONTENTS

To all the people that have never
doubted my ability and have
constantly believed in me.
To the woman who got me writing
again. This book was inspired by
our correspondence.

Prologue

I honestly do not know how I got to this point in my life. I used to be so casual about things. Nothing really mattered. I was aloof and harm would not afflict me. I believed everything would work out and it nearly always did, apart from one thing, women. I have never fully understood what makes women truly happy and content and the overwhelming complexities have always got the better of me. I know how to please a woman in the bedroom, but women are far more complicated than that. Pleasing them sexually will not give you any immunity from a woman's scorn when things go less than well. They can get angry over the slightest thing and you will spend many moments thinking about something that you may have done or did not do to upset them. And yes, mostly you will never figure out what the hell has happened at all. It will be a mystery compounded on top of all the other unexplained events where you get the cold shoulder treatment. When this happens, there are only two ways you can react. You can sulk with your annoyance and disappointment, becoming distant, or you can pacify your partner by being humble and ready to agree. Relationships are steady work and compromise and giving up on things that you want to do are part of the game in which you cede most of the social activities you like in favour of getting some bedroom action. Put simply, your animal urges are prioritized over watching a footy game or a night out with your friends. The Neanderthal who lives in all us red-blooded males is our downfall and however intelligent we like to think we are, it all comes crashing down to basic sexual needs.

Red Chapter

It used to be said that if you were born an Englishman, you had won the lottery of life, you belonged to a brave island people who single-handedly changed the demographics of the world forever. Foremost, we were a race of highly skilled mariners who navigated the globe in a quest for opportunity and fortune. The colonies we established around the world were vast and were the envy of all civilised nations. My trouble though was not with my origins, it was with my parents. My parents never took their parental roles seriously. Harry, my father, had a problem with violence and jealousy and would only be thinking about where his next drink was coming from. Jacqueline, my mother, was naive and no better than a child herself and was just seventeen when she became pregnant with a handsome boy. Children were just something that arrived and we were kind of in the way. Their battles were fierce and violent and I had a ringside seat without the popcorn. Of course, they had their moments between the wild storms where the sun shone and the birds sang, but the next downpour of domestic trouble was always lurking on the horizon. My two siblings would be far too young to remember any of this. There were no ornaments, vases or decorative items of any kind, investment in such things in a volatile environment was pointless. They had both come to realise that buying new things just to see them get broken up was a financial waste they could ill afford. The writing was on the wall that they would break up, it was just a question of when. They hoped that their situation would change for the better and save them. The breaks sadly never arrived and the violence escalated in an ominous chain of disappointments.

I was a little over 6 years old when my parents suddenly but not surprisingly separated, which led to me being placed in a children's home in Liverpool. I don't remember much about this time, or even how long I was there, but it must have been at least 2 years or more. Some things are best forgotten. My time here would drag relentlessly like a never-ending eternity of despair. I do remember that some of the staff were quite brutal in the way they treated me and others. I dreaded evening bathtime which was a daily ordeal. I was manhandled by a large evil woman who would bend me at will. She would then proceed to rub soap into my eyes and mouth, taking no notice of any obvious discomfort that was being inflicted. Struggling was futile and would only get you a dunking and more persecution. This was not a place of happiness or mercy and there was nobody to run to for comfort. It was just me, copping it sweet and crying myself to sleep. Many of the events that I witnessed and endured here have been repressed from my memory, I think for my own sanity. I do believe that this place would have broken me completely if I had stayed here. As things were, I was closer to being broken than the happy boy I once was when I arrived. A part of me had died here and was lost forever never to return. The severity of inhumanity was too much for anyone to bear, let alone a small child and it would take many years to heal and recover from. Fortunately for me, I was moved to a convent in Hammersmith, London. Divine intervention had saved me and the wretch that I had become. Hallelujah.

Hammersmith Convent was a very large old building with the smell of disinfectant running through the corridors and large marble stairways. The nuns were meticulous in their cleaning regime with all offending dirt particles eradicated on a daily basis. There was an order and a routine that had to be conformed to. After I had been at the convent for a few weeks, there was real concern that something was drastically wrong with me. I was withdrawn and not socially active. My words were very few and I would always sit on my own sometimes rocking with my back against the wall. At some point, they decided to get specialists involved and I was assigned my very own social worker who I saw once a week. I was monitored, observed, evaluated and many reports were written on my state of mind and strange behaviour. They wanted to coax me out of my safe comfort zone, but I wasn't ready and I wouldn't let them. I needed time and lots of it. I was visited by psychologists, psychiatrists and behavioural therapists in an attempt to solve my problems. What they didn't get was it wouldn't go away just because they said it was OK, I needed a calm environment and new interactions and memories to replace the bad ones which were still present and pervasive. All this would not happen quickly. They even made me sit a series of tests and puzzles to assess my mental abilities and I kind of enjoyed doing them. I knew I wasn't stupid and I revelled in showing them my true genius. I was given an IQ score on most of the tests which suggested that I was good enough to be a doctor at the very least. On another occasion, I was taken to a small hospital unit where I had electrodes placed and stuck on my forehead and my brain impulses were monitored on graph paper. I would be shown cards with pictures on them and asked what they reminded me of in order to see if my brain was working properly. Of course it was, I was just very reserved. The visits eventually became fewer and much reduced and in the end, I was only seeing my social worker every three months. I was very fortunate to convince the specialists that I was OK and more importantly sane, as they had real powers over what would happen to me. They could have signed a few papers and I would have been dispatched and banished to the far side of the country, probably forever. My intelligence and reasoning had saved me from a murky existence which I did not deserve, desire, nor want.

For a very long time, things were quiet for me and I was unnoticed and out of view. I made no waves and I was starting to settle into a routine. I was even confident enough to suck the cream off the silver top milk bottles, carefully reattaching the foil tops after a crafty mid-morning raid. However, I was still a loner with low self-esteem who was slowly re-emerging back to some kind of normality. My self-belief was only now beginning to return to me after a long absence. The prolonged spell of anonymity was helping me considerably in my recovery. There were many really good caring people working at the convent and it was a good place to recover from the torment of Liverpool. The nuns were strict, but they were also fair in their judgements and I never felt resentful of any decisions they made concerning me.

The nuns slept in dorms the same as the kids and the section where they were was strictly off bounds to anyone else, especially us. This was the great unknown place where angels fear to tread, I was the fool who just had to find out what all the fuss was about. So one evening I sneaked in to satisfy my curiosity and all I could see were curtains, like a hospital ward. I then slowly and quietly pulled up a stool and stood on it. As I peered over the curtains there was a nun undressing and at this point, I should have probably gone away. It was a young shapely nun who could have easily been a centerfold. She was curvaceous in all the right places and I was just transfixed in wonderment wanting to see more of her and watching the layers peel away. Finally, she was naked for a glorious moment before her gown went on. Her breasts firm and her nipples erect. She was a vision of beauty that no man would probably ever see. I was bowled over by her sensuality and this was truly the first time I had experienced wanting a woman. How had I turned up at this precise and opportune moment? It was as if it had been ordained. I felt very privileged and the short stolen vision of her has always stayed with me. I made my escape silently with her image running through my impressionable mind. I would never visit again, but I would dream of her often.

The nuns on the whole were quite decent and relaxed with the joy of God in their hearts. But as with any organization, there will always be a few sadists that slip through the vetting procedure and they will take great pleasure in the torment of others. Sadly for me, I was taught to eat nicely by one. A well-upholstered nun who would hold a large serving spoon above me in readiness to strike. If I ate with my mouth open, even just slightly, the spoon would be driven down until it struck the top of my head. After a few weeks or so of going to bed with bumps on my head. I finally became the perfect eater, always keeping my lips tightly together when chewing. The punishment spoon no longer hovered over me and had moved on to find another unsuspecting victim. One week, I had been very disobedient and I was becoming unruly. The nuns were struggling to control me. I was bigger and far more confident in my own abilities. But the nuns had a cunning plan and this took the form of a confession box. I never knew what their purpose was and always thought they were just for adults. I had never seen a child go in one. They were dark and austere, they also looked scary and uninviting. So when I was escorted by two nun mountains to a confession box, my heart started to race. I was placed on a wooden seat and the curtain drawn on me. It was dark and there was a musty smell. My eyes started to adjust to the poor light. My heart was still racing and the fear of not knowing what was going to happen was not helping. Suddenly a voice from nowhere came quick and loud.

"Confess your sins child," the voice said.

which really freaked me out and perturbed me. I was so scared I confessed to all the dastardly bad things I did that week. This took some time as there was a lot to divulge and this didn't even include taking a gander at a young nun. Eventually, I finished blubbing and I sat there sorrowful and awaited my fate. I was sure it would be severe and I would deserve it. After a long silence which seemed to last forever, the voice came back quick and loud with the verdict.

"Now child, say three hail marys and two our fathers and be gone with you," the voice said.

The curtain was pulled open and the nun mountains escorted me away. I was impressed and relieved with the forgiving nature of my punishment and vowed to be good in return. I would make my peace with the nuns and become an exemplary pupil of high merit. It would not last for long. Only a near-death experience would change my behaviour and that was to happen very soon.

The convent was a big imposing Victorian building over five floors and the children were all situated on the fourth floor. It was the only floor with a balcony which hugged the building on three sides and was large enough to accommodate a children's play area. This had a wire fence on a wall on the open side that was rounded on the top to stop anyone climbing up. As with all things you shouldn't do, there is always some idiot that will do it, and on this day that idiot was me, I climbed the fence with ease and lay across it with my stomach on the rounded part. My head was now peeking over and looking right down over four floors. If this wasn't insane enough I then started to swing the wire fence backwards and forwards. after an unknown amount of swings, my balance was wrong and I felt my stomach turn over. I was going over. I quickly stretched my legs backwards and remained motionless, still slightly off balance. My hands were gripping the fence near my knees and they would not hold me if my body flipped over. I needed to do something quickly. So using my hands I started to pull my body ever so slowly back from the brink, keeping my legs stretched behind me. I kept thinking, not now, not now, please not now. It was working, and with every millimetre gained the feeling of terror started to fade. When my two feet touched the balcony I was shaking all over. I felt both relief and exhilaration. I had cheated death and won the prize of my existence. This was a second chance. I would be good and the nuns would like me again. This has changed me for the better, I think. But the winds of change were already in the air and after five and a half years the nuns had given up on me. In their eyes, I was a heathen who had not absorbed any of their teachings. My behaviour was getting more erratic and turbulent. Disruption in the convent had to be dealt with and they had made their decision. They would now place me in the hands of the enemy. A protestant Church of England boarding school in the green county of leafy Surrey. This would be my renaissance, where the caterpillar is remarkably transformed in its ability, purpose and habitat.

Green Chapter

In English society when I was growing up, boarding schools were known for being elitist and mainly made up of pupils from middle to upper-class families. It was absolutely their preserve. The cost being so high that it would prohibit anyone else from attending one of these glorious establishments. I, however, had been deemed a special case by social workers and government finance would be paying my way. Every year the local authority would pick up the tab for my stay, which was fine by me. Here I would excel in ways I never dreamed possible. I would be popular and it would make me the person I am today.

I arrived in the summer with the shimmer of bright light all around me, as if I was an angel descended from the heavens. But, I fell far short of being angelic. I was me and I felt dissimilar somehow from others of my age, with my own unique set of values. I was certainly different, but I could not be categorised or predicted. I was neither fish nor fowl. I was an unknown quantity and the flag of who I was and what I stood for had not been hoisted for everyone to see. I was still forming opinions on many things in an analytical and rational way, but my character and principles were already formed and they would govern my thinking and my interaction with others.

I was feeling good and the wonderful sunny weather seemed to intensify my first impressions of Outwood Manor School. As I arrived I stared up at the splendour of this beautiful school. The front of the main building was built with grey stone blocks which had been added to over the years with brick extensions.

The front door was very large and imposing with grand Romanesque columns on either side. When I arrived I was ushered into the headmaster's office and given a brief history of the school and its traditions. This was quickly followed by an extensive talk on school rules which made me sleepy with my eyelids growing very heavy. The headmaster was pleasant and was well versed in dealing with new entrants. There were many gleaming silver cups and shields on display that the school had won over the years. on one of the shelves, there was a collection of canes and slippers which I would get to know intimately at a later date. I was then given a tour of the school by one of the Housemasters and was amazed at the grand scale of this place. The grounds alone stretched as far as my eyes could see. It made Hammersmith look like a shoebox. There were many dorms (dormitories) for all ages up till 18. Girls and boys were segregated and had their own dorms. There was a large dining hall, an on-site sick ward with a Matron and her mankiller milk monsters. A

Seamstress to look after your clothing. This place was vast. It even had its own church. Amen. I was then shown around my dorm which was called Robin Dorm. All the dorms were named after birds. It had about 30 beds which were spread around the dorm about 3 feet apart in a horseshoe shape. Old and worn varnished floorboards were everywhere and polished to a high shine. I would collect many splinters from these accursed floorboards over the coming years.

It took a few days for my shyness to subside and to start settling in and integrating with my other classmates. But once I got going there was no stopping me. I found out that all the pupils were very well mannered and would never swear or speak out of turn. They were soft and had never known hardship or brutality the way I had. I was the black sheep and they respected and feared me to the same extent. In a short space of time, there had been a bloodless coup and now there was a new top dog of Robin Dorm. I was the new undisputed king and I was in control. The crown firmly on my head and not even a sniff of a rival.

When you're in a boarding school there are always some pupils that are just way too annoying to be ignored. They will be disliked by everyone because they run against the grain. They celebrate in being an irritation to all that come into contact with them. Some will even enjoy being beaten and will do what it takes to achieve this and get their daily dose. Some just have no dignity at all and will masturbate and cry out loud when they shoot their load. Consideration for others is not on the agenda. It is self-gratification all the way and fuck everyone else. In a dorm of 30 beds, you can't have much self-esteem to behave in this way. One pupil in particular called Kirk would do a five knuckle shuffle every night. He would cry out with wild abandonment, and the impact on his bed neighbours was damaging them psychologically. They were pleading with me every day to do something about it. We all knew it went on, but mostly it was in a discreet way and kept quiet. Kirk was another beast, he was full-on and left nothing to the imagination. Eventually, I came onside when he started spanking the monkey twice a night. Every evening we would get reading time of 30 minutes before lights out. So we used this time to plan our assault. On this night we were ready and waiting to take action. At least 15 of us would be involved in Operation Stop Spanking The Monkey. Finally, the lights went out and they waited for me to make the first move. I wanted things to settle and the quiet of night to set in before I proceeded. It became very quiet, apart from some cover pounding coming from Kirk's bed. I made my way over as nearly all the dorm arrived at his bedside in a united declaration of anger and disgust. We made our move and his arms and feet were held as Chinese burns were administered to them with everyone having a turn. He was screaming, but his mouth was covered by someone's hands so only muffled shrieks were audible. Toothpaste was squeezed in generous amounts into his eyes and hair and rubbed in for good measure. He was then given a few slaps and told to be quiet from now on. He really looked a mess. At this point, we all left him and returned to our beds. For some reason after leaving him in a quiet state, Kirk decided to throw a hissy fit. He was screaming at the top of his voice and rolling around the floor in an erratic way, like an unbalanced lunatic. This alerted the Housemaster who immediately came to his aid. Then a second Housemaster arrived. All the lights were on and everyone was being questioned over Kirk's appearance and how he got this way. He looked like a toothpaste victim of the highest order and would surely receive a gold medal position for looking so tragic and ruined. If only the Housemasters knew why this had happened. We were all keeping quiet and none of us was helping in any way. We were united in our cause and would not crack under pressure. Kirk was also keeping quiet with the help of a few hard looks. He knew he would be ostracised and life would be made very difficult for him. The Housemasters had a conundrum. They needed to punish somebody to show that things like this cannot happen without penalties. There was no evidence, not even from Kirk. But he didn't get into this mess all on his own. Something would have to be done. It was decided after much discussion that every fifth boy would visit the Headmaster's office. I was one of the lucky six to be marched down the long dimly lit corridor and await punishment. I would be the first to go so I had no idea what to expect. The Headmaster was in his pyjamas and dressing gown and not looking very happy. It was all very simple really. Just bend over the chair, buttocks out and brace yourself for six of the best. Headmaster selected a slipper from his box of tricks and got himself into position. My hands were held behind my back with the blows arriving soon after. They landed one after another until the pain train had reached its destination, Deter and Dissuade. When we had all been on our pain journeys, we were returned back to the dorm. It would be a mostly peaceful night with some occasional feverish, frenzied, cover pounding.

Events always unfold in an unpredictable way and whilst I was enjoying my new-found status as leader of Robin Dorm, dark clouds were gathering around me. Trouble was to come from an unlikely source and from literally nowhere. I was walking down the corridor with two friends when I was tripped from behind by an older boy who was 2 years above me. I gave him some backchat to save some face, But because of this, he would remember me. And so it began. Every time he would see me, it would be a punch in the arm or back, tripping me up or just name-calling to undermine and erode my position. This guy was like a fly that just kept coming back at you no matter how much you tried to get rid of it. Drastic measures would have to be implemented to resolve this situation in my favour. It had to show everyone that nobody pushes Paul around, not even the older kids. They would learn to respect me and give me a wide berth because I was unpredictable, and this would give me an advantage over all who would face me. A plan was set which would make me look good and most importantly, I would avoid a beating. After all, he was way bigger than me and if given the right opportunity, I would be an invalid for life. His size would have to be respected and no chances would be given. The next day I avoided him all morning till lunchtime. Everyone was here and the scene was set. I sat two tables behind him on his blind side and kept myself low. I had my lunch on a tray but I couldn't eat. I was too busy psyching myself up for my intended assault. Everything was set with two teachers near to where he was sitting. I had to use my fists only. Anything else and I would face being expelled from the school. I stood up with my intentions set and my target confirmed. I made my way over and was standing right behind him. I waited. Everyone must see me. He turned his head and I knew this was my moment. My first punch was moving before he even registered that it was me. I caught him so well that he went over sideways off his chair like a good sturdy English Oak. I then threw his half-eaten meal over him while he was in recovery mode. This was perfect. I jumped in and rained punches down on him until I was pulled off by a shocked teacher. I watched as they pulled him up off the floor in a dishevelled state. He was visibly shaking and did not make eye contact with me. Everyone was silent. They all knew now what I was capable of if angered and nobody would ever look sideways at me again. There was only one place we were going now, and that was straight to the Headmaster's office where we would both give our versions of events. When my turn came, I told the Headmaster that I was being bullied and I had to stop it. I also said that punching him back was just a small fraction of what he had done to me on the quiet. I think the Headmaster had a sneaking admiration for standing up to bullies because our punishment was exactly the same. So, as well as taking a beating at dinner the Big Bull would now face the cane across the knuckles as well. Plus a warning that a bigger punishment would be delivered if there were any more incidents with Paul. I could have kissed the Headmaster. He had come down unequivocally on my side. Just by looking at us, you could see it was an unequal contest in size and girth. A true David and Goliath contest with David triumphant once again. This plan had turned out even better than I had ever imagined. But as I was rejoicing in my head, the Big Bull came out of the office with tears streaming down his face. He was utterly broken and finished as a force and would never bother anyone again. It was my turn and I vowed not to cry like Big Bull. If I didn't cry, they would be talking about this for years. How the big guy was crying like a baby and Paul came out unaffected and brave. I held my hands out, knuckles up, As the cane struck, I could feel excruciating pain, which just on its own would make your eyes water. After 5 strikes I was on my knees. My eyes were streaming but no noise. I stood and got my composure back, wiped my eyes dry and walked towards the door.

I was halfway good but not brave and strong. They would still talk about this for years, as events like this were rare and the performance was spectacular. I was the king and respect had been restored.

At this time I was a big tree climber and would think nothing of scaling a tree 100 feet tall (30 meters). Going up was easy and I was audacious and unflinching in my fearless ascent. But coming down was way more perilous with the distance between me and the ground clearly defined. I never did like heights, but I somehow conquered my fears by following my brave friends and not being a pussy. We were left to our own devices and climbing trees was an everyday occurrence. Sometimes we would go up the same tree in small groups of 4 to 5 and when we reached the top, we would have a smoking party and chat and laugh about things happening in the school. Health and Safety was in its infancy and we were expected to do these things and be boisterous. So, one Sunday after playing football, a group of us went over to the woods, which was close to the football pitch. There was a game that we played and it was for serious adrenaline junkies only. We would scale pine trees which are well known for their flexibility. We would then climb to the very top and start swaying from side to side in an attempt to get the biggest swing in a death-defying game of insanity. This was great, we were all flying from side to side with no thought of any impending jeopardy. We were all overdosing on the thrill and excitement of our perilous manoeuvres. Little did I know that danger was imminent and ready to capitalize on my mindless behaviour. I heard something snap. Next thing I knew, I was hurtling towards the ground face down taking all the branches out from one side of the tree as I fell. I hit the ground in a prone position with all of my front side hitting at once. The most terrifying thing was that I had just missed a freshly cut pine tree stump with a point on it, which was on my left side. Just a foot to the left and I would have been impaled. I had been thoroughly winded with all the air pushed from my chest and I was trying very hard to breathe again. Nothing was happening. I struggled to a clearing still not breathing with pins and needles all over my body. I fell to the ground. This was it. This would be where life leaves my body. As I lay there expecting the end, I began very slowly to shallow breathe. It was still not enough, but it was something. I stayed very still trying not to expend energy and very gradually my breathing started to return. When I could stand again, I slowly made my way back to the school building where my friends had run for help. My only injuries were a few small cuts and some grazing, but my confidence had taken a big knock. I would never climb large trees again. Just small ones.

I was developing a reputation for being indestructible, and walking away from a massive tree fall was making its way swiftly around the school. This and the Big Bull incident were propelling me to new heights. I was looked upon as some kind of unbreakable entity who was shadowed by a guardian angel. I was very careful not to let all this go to my head. I detested and despised arrogant people and would never allow myself to become one. Humility was in my heart, I believed everyone had their nemesis and to be mindful of this is a great leveller. Moreover, the tree itself became an attraction, and everyone would come to see how far I had fallen. They would look in disbelief at the huge height and all the broken branches and wonder how the hell I had survived without any serious injury.

Saturday morning pictures were a big event here. Every week all the students would walk two abreast down the long school road and into the town nearly half a mile away. Girl with girl, boy with boy. Our numbers were large and the cinema was always full. We were escorted by our Housemasters and Housemistresses who would sit through the showing with us and keep order. On the whole, we were well behaved as this was something we enjoyed and we didn't want to lose the privilege. Sometimes we would have an old movie premier and one, in particular, stood out for me. It was One Million Years BC with Raquel Welch. The male character in this film called Tumak was escaping a primitive and barbaric existence with his own tribe of savages. He became an outcast and after a long journey, happened upon another tribe that looked after him. He saw that they were living in a much more civilized and harmonious way. I could instantly see the parallel between my own existence and the character of Tumak in his struggle for a better life. It was on these excursions that I began to notice a girl called Sarah, whom I developed a crush on. She was so beautiful with her long blonde hair and if she didn't have our love child, my life would surely be over. But in reality, I would be content just to kiss her and feel her soft skin against mine.

Life went on for a while with the seasons rolling by, and with every glimpse of Sarah, my feelings would grow stronger. I also continued to flout the rules. And on this occasion, I was caught scrolling "Knock 4

Love" on a sealed up corridor door by one of the Housemistresses, for which I had to serve a detention. It was a bit immature but it was also funny and I wanted to share it. As she was busy with her dorm looking after the girls, the detention would be served there, in Nightingale Dorm. This was Sarah's dorm. As I walked in with the Housemistress, I became very aware of being an object of scrutiny, like I was a major showcase exhibit. All the girls were staring at me and smiling. I began to feel a little nervous with so much attention, but I held my nerve and managed to smile back. The Housemistress told all the girls to carry on getting ready and to ignore me.

"Sit down over there Paul and cover your eyes," she said.

I was made to sit down on the floor in the middle of the dorm with my arms on my knees and my face down on my arms, so I couldn't see the girls getting ready for bed. I could hear the girls laughing and whispering things about me. This was great. I would have paid to be here, and here I was, my bad behaviour rewarded. I put my chin on my knees and my hands over my eyes but I was leaving a slight gap between my fingers. I could see everything and they didn't even know. Sarah was giggling with her friend and shaking her bum in her loose nighty. They both kept looking over at me. Maybe I had a chance, maybe she did like me. I was having a feel-good moment. Everything seemed possible and my dreams were alive. But before I could put any plan into action, I was struck down with a sty which flared up the very next morning. And just like that, I was in the Sick Ward all on my own.

My sty became a big problem and had spread to both eyes. They were very sore and in the mornings were welded together. Antiseptic creams were used in my treatment and I lost many weeks stuck in the Sick Ward with Matron and her mankiller milk monsters. I could see my friends all queuing on Saturday mornings for the cinema and would wave at them from my window on the ground floor. My friends and even

Sarah would wave back. They missed me and I missed them too. My life was on hold until I was well again. Towards the end of my stay with my eyes nearly healed a new patient arrived with a swollen ankle and was placed in the bed opposite. It was Sarah. She waved as Matron attended to her. I waved back with a large grin. There was a god and he did love me. Life could only be bad for so long before something good comes along, which will raise you up again. For so long I had wanted to escape the confines of this ward and return to my friends, but now Sarah was here I wanted to stay. Suddenly there was joy in this place and hope had arrived. I waited for Matron to finish applying her bandage. I then walked towards her bed. We had never spoken before.

So when I said "Fancy playing hangman."

She replied, "I'd love to Paul."

I couldn't believe my ears. She actually knew my name and here I was making myself comfortable sitting on her bed with the ruse of playing hangman. Now I was close up with her, she looked even more gorgeous. Good job we were playing a game, otherwise, Matron would definitely ask me to go back to my bed. This was great. I didn't even care if I won or lost, I was sitting next to the prettiest girl in the school. I thought of a word and marked lines on the paper with an X under each vowel. And we started. She looked so happy to be playing hangman. Her first five letters had all failed to register and we both laughed at her inability to find even one. I had a plan though and even she wouldn't lose. I would give the hangman fingers and toes. I was studying her more closely and our eyes did not divert. There was no shyness and we were completely at ease in each other's company. She finally got the word without dying. The word was "Princess." She laughed, she knew that I meant her. We played on for an hour or so with our laughter getting louder and our proximity getting closer until Matron told us it was nearly bedtime. Which meant, brush your teeth and get ready for bed.

When the lights went out. we stayed awake and whispered into the night. She soon asked me if I wanted to be her boyfriend, and I told her how much I really wanted her to be my girlfriend until my eyes grew heavy and I fell asleep. It was not to last. I was woken by someone moving my arm. It was Sarah.

"I didn't say goodnight properly," she said.

I sat up. She was looking into my eyes with no distance between us. We both moved together until our lips touched. Then we kissed for the first time like two students of love. It was instinctual and neither one of us knew what we were doing. But it felt good and I didn't want it to end. Eventually, we paused and embraced for a while, Then she smiled affectionately and whispered goodnight.

"Wait, let me help you," I said

I then helped her back to her bed and covered her up. I kissed her on the forehead, as it shows you care, respect, and probably love if you kiss someone in this way. I returned to my bed and laid back and closed my eyes. Was it possible to be this fulfilled and content? As excited as I was, my tiredness was much greater and I was quickly taken by the night.

Purple Chapter

The next day I opened my eyes and Sarah was sitting up in bed looking pretty and smiling at me.

"Good morning Paul," she said.

I smiled, pulled the sheet up over my head and then revealed myself again.

"Hi Sarah," I replied.

I felt like I could walk on water. I was so lucky to have her so interested in me. Maybe I was selling myself short. Perhaps, I too had something to offer. It is a human condition to self-doubt even when things are going so well, but for now, it was kept to the back of my mind. I told Sarah I would be back soon and went to the washroom to freshen up. Matron would be doing her rounds soon. My eyes looked OK and I wondered how long I would have left with Sarah. The good thing about being sick is that you stay in your pyjamas. No need to change, just like a sofa day. I combed my hair and air-kissed towards the mirror, then went back to Sarah. It would be hard to beat yesterday. I was chatting with Sarah from my bed when Matron entered the ward. I didn't want to be seen at her bed without a good reason. Matron examined Sarah first and I heard her say at least another 3 days for the swelling to go down. Sarah smiled in my direction, but I was not feeling so confident. I gave my eyes a rub to make them look a bit sorer. Matron then strolled towards me and smiled.

"Now Paul, I bet you don't want to go now young beauty is opposite," Matron said.

Did Matron know something, maybe she saw us kissing or maybe it was good intuition or just a hunch. But now I was looking over at Sarah I realized that it would take a complete moron not to notice that she was totally besotted and under my spell. If Matron knew about us, she would have to send me back to the dorm, to separate us. It would be her duty for the good of the school. She looked over my eyes and turned my head to the light.

"Still a little red, looks like you two will have 2 more days together," Matron said with a smile.

I could barely believe my ears. She knows we like each other and she's not sending me back. Matron is a true romantic and is fanning the flames of love by keeping us together. I now saw Matron in a different light. She was liberal on matters of the heart and definitely on my team and Sarah's. This was our time, because once we were both back in our dorms our opportunities to see each other unsupervised will be limited. We would get time together in after school association, but this would be supervised. How much actual supervising they did was debatable, but they were still there. Breakfast, dinner, supper, church, assembly, we will only be able to glance at each other. but seeing her smile and passing the odd love letter will still mean something. Not to mention my standing with my classmates, to whom having a girlfriend is an aspiration. Also, you cannot sneak into the girl's dorms at night because they are locked to stop any hanky-panky. So the two of us in opposite beds on our own, mostly unsupervised, really is a big deal, and Matron is a revelation and a godsend.

We started our day after breakfast with a game of operation. For anyone not familiar with this game you basically take a card and it will give you a prize of money for successfully removing an ailment from Cavity Sam with a pair of tweezers. If Cavity Sams's nose lights up red and a buzzer sounds you fail. If you succeed, you will be paid the amount on the card and the next player will play. You need a steady hand to be good at this, so I let Sarah go first. Surprisingly her first operation was good and she received her prize money. She waved her money at me and revelled in her achievement. Her smile was infectious and I too became overjoyed in her ecstatic state of celebration, for which I received a big hug. On my turn my hands were steady but I had no desire to outplay Sarah. When the nose lit up and the buzzer sounded I acted like I was disappointed. This affected Sarah to the point of feeling sorry for me. The next thing I knew, she had her arms around me again in consolation. I liked her touchy-feely nature and she had no problem expressing her adoration for me. For my part, I just enjoyed the feeling of being loved and someone holding me. What Sarah didn't know was that all my life until now I had been starved of love and nobody had held me before in an affectionate way. Her love was feeding a hidden craving that had laid dormant within me and had never been sustained. Her love was empowering me. It was setting me free from all those years of misery and torment. That barren bleak existence in my early years.

waiting to be rescued with help never arriving. None of this was important anymore. Her love was making it all fade away and I was feeling whole again. Sunshine and affection were filling my life and I had been elevated. I felt brighter and I could see my path ahead. I had a chance.

As for the game, we had both lost interest with Sarah way ahead and holding all the money. I had made it too easy for her and there was no competition. The simple truth was we were both waiting for the night to come around again so we could practice and perfect our kissing techniques and as the hours went by the anticipation was reaching boiling point. We did not speak about it. We just knew it was going to happen because there was a need within both of us to continue what we had started. As bedtime approached we both became more serious and less playful. We were comfortable in our silence just gazing at each other with longing desire. Matron finally made her call for bedtime in her usual cheerful manner and we both brushed our teeth and got into bed. We said goodnight to Matron and then to each other and the lights went out. After a little time had passed Sarah whispered my name and asked me to go to her. I needed no persuasion, her lure was too great. We were like two magnets that once attracted, would have no possibility of avoiding contact. It would definitely happen. Our impulses gave us no choice. I made my way to her bed with my eyes adjusting to the darkness and found her outstretched arm which guided me towards her. I could feel the warmth of her body and the softness of her skin as I pulled her close to me. I pressed my cheek against hers and stroked her soft hair. Her heart was beating hard and her breathing was intense. My mouth made it's way slowly down her cheek until our lips engaged in a rendezvous of passion. I pressed against her as our lips stroked gently and lovingly. I couldn't help thinking how well we were doing this and how good it felt. We were losing our amateur status and were becoming accomplished and talented in the art of kissing. I started wetting her lips with my tongue so they moved more freely across mine in a rhythmic motion. She was enjoying this as much as me. My hands were caressing and navigating her body as we kissed. We were taking it slow and savouring every lingering moment and our heightened senses were capturing every signal of pleasure. We paused for a moment and gazed at each other. She was running her fingers softly over the contours of my face and smiling at me. She then playfully pulled at my ear, I reacted by kissing her again but this time with more urgency. My tongue pushed its way between her lips and began exploring her mouth. Our tongues then engaged in encounter after encounter, in an arousing bout of skirmishes. I felt a tingling sensation stirring in my groin which I had never encountered before. Something was happening to me and I was rock hard. I wanted to do unspeakable things to Sarah but I couldn't because I respected her too much and would never harm her in any way. She was my princess. The weight of responsibility was weighing heavy on me to be strong and to do the right thing. So, for now, I would wrestle with this problem on my own. Eventually, I held Sarah for a while and then returned to my bed. What was happening to me, every time my penis touched something the tingling sensation would return. I was restless and I couldn't sleep and I was thinking about Sarah and all the immoral depraved things that I wanted to do to her. I turned forward and faced the mattress with my penis pressing against it. It was tingling again, this time, even more. It became rigid again and very hard. I imagined Sarah was under me as I started to press against the mattress with my now enlarged erection. I was pushing hard at it with the pleasure sensation increasing with each push. I couldn't stop. I was on a one-way mission to an unknown destination and it felt tremendous. It was getting hot down there and things were definitely reaching a crescendo with all gauges in the red. The touchpaper had been ignited and something was going to blow.

Suddenly, a massive surge rushed through my penis. It felt like I was unloading in bucket loads and it also felt like the whole bed was wet through and drenched. What would Matron say in the morning, not to mention Sarah's thoughts on the subject? But when I scrambled around the mattress feeling the sheets, they were dry. It was just wet in a very small patch. An embarrassing situation had been avoided. It really felt like I had urinated over the whole bed, but I hadn't. I learned at a later age that this was a wet dream which most teenagers go through. Girls in a different way which I won't explain. I stopped panicking and laid back in bed, closed my eyes and began to think deeply. Sarah and I were the same age. Maybe she had been through a similar experience just like me. I thought some more and soon my thoughts gradually turned to dreams, that quickly propelled the night into morning.

I woke up to:

"Good morning sleepyhead."

It was Matron and she was doing her rounds. I pulled the cover over my head still half asleep, but there was no escape. She needed to see my eyes. So when she pulled the cover down, I cooperated and obliged with her tasks. I had come to like Matron and did not want to upset her.

"Looking very good Paul. should be good to go tomorrow," she said.

I thought about my friends and how glad they would be to see me and how I had missed being around them. A sadness came over me with the realization that my time in the ward with Sarah was coming to an end. I looked over at Sarah and she waved. I smiled back to keep her happy, but it was veiled and was hiding my true sorrow. After Matron had gone Sarah called me over. I shuffled over with my slippers half on and held her hand. But before I could speak, she said:

"What were you doing in your bed yesterday."

I had been found out and I really didn't know what to say. I genuinely did not want to talk about it at all. I was embarrassed and I was also busted. What could I say to her that would make it all disappear? Maybe I could say I was having some kind of a fit or convulsion or maybe there was a wasp under the sheets which caused me to move so frantically. Would any of these excuses convince her? Probably not, she was way too clever to fall for sorry excuses. So I just said:

"I don't think you will understand."

It would at least buy me some more time to conjure up an excuse. She gave me a hard look and said:

"How can you say that, just tell me the truth."

This was serious, I was boxed in a corner with no possible way out. She would either hate me forever or she will forgive my misdemeanour. This was our first bump in the road and there was a real possibility I could lose her. It was like I was in a confession box all over again with way more on the line. But I also remembered how forgiving they were and the good feeling of unburdening my secrets. Can the truth really set you free? I was about to find out. I made myself comfortable still holding her hand and I had to lower my voice and whisper. I began to tell her about all the things that I wanted to do to her and that I didn't think she was ready. I also told her about my experience yesterday in my bed which I explained in great detail even saying that I imagined her under me. I then awaited my fate. It was a lot to comprehend and I could see she was thinking hard about what to say. She then squeezed my hand. That must be a good sign. If it was bad she would push my hand away. She then told me that she was glad I had been honest and that she really liked me. She wanted to take things slowly and we could also think about doing other things together for now. I didn't know what she had in mind but this was responsible stuff and this was why I liked her. She was intelligent and beautiful. She also knew now what was in my head and how I was thinking. It was no longer a dark secret to be ashamed of. She had accepted my explanation and made some compromises and would continue to be my girlfriend. I felt much better now and we still had another night. We watched a lot of telly on the last day. We sat on the sofa together secretly holding hands under a pillow and just enjoying being close. Occasionally kissing when Matron was out of range. Once back in our dorms, these moments would have to be worked for and stolen. So, for now, we enjoyed our privileged autonomy from school formalities. Matron would appear sporadically to see if things were OK. On her last visit, noticing that we had not moved for a long time.

"Are you two lovebirds still sitting there," she said. We both smiled. I'm sure Matron had an inkling that something was amiss. I mean really, just the way we looked at each other was a giveaway. We had both come to rely on Matron's easy-going nature. She kept the secret of our warm attachment and we were confident it would go no further. We had probably done way more than even Matron could imagine us doing. But for now, we were trusted and any doubts dispelled. We were getting bored with the telly and decided to play hangman. The game that brought us together. This time I was guessing and Sarah was now laughing at me. I was useless but I just got in under the wire. The word was "Boyfriend."

"So you have a boyfriend? Why didn't anyone tell me?" I said.

She gave me her hard look again then smiled, she got the joke. She leaned over and kissed me.

"You. Silly," she said.

Shortly after this, Matron came around with two glasses of milk and a tin of biscuits on a tray. She was great. I won't get pampered like this tomorrow. If there was a point in time where you could just stop the clock and stay in that moment, this would be it. Nothing could reach the pinnacle of the last 3 days, could it? After devouring the Custard Creams, Orange Creams, Jammy Dodgers and Bourbons we continued with Hangman. It was Sarah's turn to guess and I wanted to get some kind of reaction from her. The word was set and she was cruising. She had got good at this. I didn't even get to the rope when she had the answer. It was "Mattress." But she looked furious.

"I can't believe you put that. you can't replace me with a fucking mattress!" she said angrily.

I was taken aback by the hostility in her voice and in her face. This had really upset her and I hadn't seen that till now. I had never heard her swear or anyone else in the school. She was quietly sobbing with teardrops streaming down her cheeks. I instantly felt remorse for my actions and my thoughtlessness. I hurried to comfort her and held her close to me. I could feel her tears all over my cheek and down my neck, she was really upset.

"I'm so sorry, I didn't know it would have this effect on you," I said.

She was delicate, like a flower and I needed to remember that. I stroked her hair softly in a calming motion. Her sobbing was easing and her tears had stopped. I rocked her gently and all was quiet apart from the occasional sniffle.

"Here, let me fix you up," I said.

I wiped her cheeks with the sleeves of my pyjamas and tidied her hair.

"There, you're beautiful again," I said.

She smiled and looked up at me and then she said it.

"I love you, Paul. and I'll do anything for you."

This really meant something. Nobody had ever loved me before. I had no recollection of my parents loving me which had all been lost in the sands of time. I loved her too and I told her, but this was uncharted territory for me and I had mixed emotions. I was overjoyed that she loved me, but I was also a little scared, as I remembered my parent's fights. We abandoned hangman and I went to get a blanket. I came back and draped the blanket around her and we snuggled up with it on the sofa and watched some more telly. We were mindful of Matron but were not overly concerned as we were just relaxing and behaving ourselves. The evening was drawing in and the light was starting to dwindle. I looked up at Sarah and she was running her tongue over her lips suggestively. She was way ahead of me, I was still in shock over her reaction to the mattress episode. Maybe I had given her too much information on a very personal event which should have remained a secret. Perhaps she felt rejected because it wasn't with her and I could certainly understand that. I gestured "No," silently with my mouth, but I could not hold back a smile before I covered my eyes to hide my awkwardness. This was a side of Sarah I had not seen before and her confidence and execution were making me uneasy. Just a short while ago she was a sobbing wreck in need of consoling. Now she was transformed into a calculated manipulator. After seeing her worst side perhaps all her inhibitions had disappeared. I would need to be strong for the night that lay ahead, but I had serious doubts about resisting something that I desired and wanted.

Later that evening Matron gave the call to get ready for bed. I was feeling a little nervous as I brushed my teeth. Sarah was smiling but was not looking at me, like she knew something that I didn't. We made our way back to our beds and we all said our goodnights. Matron flicked the light switch and the ward was dark. I lay there with my eyes open allowing them to adjust to the dark. I had a feeling that events were already out of my control and Sarah's newfound prowess would dominate my own weaknesses. She was waiting longer tonight, allowing the anticipation to build. Expectancy was also building in my pyjamas like a monument of desire locked and loaded and ready for action. Of course, I had no control over this and being in this state was making my resistance pitiful at best. I then noticed she was slowly making her way over. Her silhouette looked more shapely than usual, as she got closer her nighty was missing and she was naked. So this was why she was smiling. She had lost all fears of any consequences and was only focused on our last night. She was also willing to sacrifice everything for this moment. What kind of a person would I be if I abandoned our love, in favour of following the rules and being safe? Love makes you do crazy things and history is littered with many examples. In my view, she was very brave and noble and if she was going to crash and burn, then I would burn with her. I would be loyal and defend her till the very end. As she approached I stared at her figure in all its glory. I was captivated. I felt a deep yearning for her which consumed me totally. In a few short moments, I had been outflanked and overrun by a far superior force. I had no resistance. I would comply with her every need and request.

"Wait," I said.

I quickly ran to her bed and put some pillows under the sheets, so if Matron checks, she would think Sarah was there. I then returned to my bed and removed my pyjamas. I pushed the covers back and made room for Sarah and she climbed in. We moved close and embraced with our bodies locked and passing over each other. She was very warm and her skin on mine was so soft and silky smooth. She moved over me and started pushing against my penis. I was so hard and the rubbing motion was exciting me even more. It was then that I felt Sarah's hand holding it and pressing it against her. The tracks were extremely wet when the train entered the tunnel. The feeling was breathtaking as we pushed together in regular motion. We were both trying to be quiet and Sarah even had one hand over her mouth to hold back any sounds of pleasure. I was close to unloading and Sarah was lost in an inner turmoil of muffled moans and sighs. Her smell and her sweat were intoxicating. It was all over me, and in the air. It was so sensual and I was lingering in the moment. All of a sudden I had passed the point of no return and an eruption of high intensity was rushing through me. I held Sarah tightly as I released in irregular bursts. When I had finished I lay there spent and dissipated. Sarah laid against me, still joined and kissed me all over. Her fingers were touching my lips and I playfully bit them. She smiled and kissed me again. So much for taking it easy. Things had changed forever and we now had an unbreakable bond. Nobody could come between us. My thoughts turned to my departure and how I would miss being here with Sarah. This moment and being here with her and embracing was all going to be gone. We were both holding each other for as long as we could, but eventually, she returned back to her bed. We said goodnight, with the full knowledge that it may be some time till we are anywhere close to what we had just experienced.

The next morning I was woken by Sarah with a gentle kiss. It was still early and she wanted to have some time with me before I departed. We spoke nothing of the night before and focused on the here and now. She looked a little unhappy so I gave her a hug. As I was holding her she started sobbing and her emotions poured out. It was as if the act of holding her had triggered the release of her sadness.

"I will miss you so much," she said.
She then ran her tear-soaked cheek over mine.

"Hey, don't be sad, we will have many more times together. I promise you," I said.

We both smiled and I held her again. This was a promise I would endeavour to keep. She was much brighter now and more relaxed after my reassurance. She would probably be out tomorrow as her foot was much better already. Just a slight limp. We enjoyed some more time together until the moment came to get myself ready. Today would be the first day for nearly 5 weeks when I actually get to wear clothes again and rejoin my dorm. I was sitting on my bed looking dapper when Matron arrived to do her rounds. I was even having a good hair day with every strand sitting perfectly in the right place. This was a rare event as most of the time there would be a rebellious patch sticking up and wetting it would only partially control the mutinous locks.

"Good morning Paul, looking handsome today," Matron said.

I smiled as she went to examine Sarah's foot. After her examination, she told Sarah one more day.

"Have you been crying Sarah," Matron said.

The tone in Matron's voice was very sympathetic and kindly which culminated in setting Sarah off again. She was crying in Matron's arms and all I could do was look on. Matron was coping very well like a surrogate mother cradling Sarah in her arms and whispering words of comfort as she rocked her back and forth. After a while Sarah was calm and Matron said,

"So why are you so upset, Sarah? Is it because Paul is going?"

She so had her finger on the pulse. She knew everything, well I certainly hope not everything.

Sarah replied, "Yes, I will miss Paul."

There was a long silence then.

"What if I said Paul could visit when he is free. Would that cheer you up," Matron said.

Sarah threw her arms around Matron and said:

"Yes Matron, yes."

She looked so happy and the joy in her face was undeniable. She would not be alone on her last night, at least for some of the time. It was time for me to go and

Matron gave me a cuddle, she really was the best. I then walked over to Sarah and gave her a big hug. I've always disliked goodbyes, but this was not final and was much easier to deal with as I would be back later. I then said my farewells and made my way out of the ward.

Yellow Chapter

I had left the sick ward on a Saturday morning and by the time I had reached the dorm, everyone was at the cinema. I put the telly on in the common room and relaxed for a while. I was enjoying the peace and isolation in a place that was normally alive with commotion and activity. Rainbow was on the telly which I didn't care for that much. The only thing I liked in this program was when Zippy had his mouth zipped shut, normally by Bungle who would take offence from Zippy's harsh words. If you have never seen Rainbow, it was a kid's TV show. There were two cloth hand puppets (Zippy and George) always behind a desk counter to hide the puppeteers. A guy in a bear suit (Bungle) and a mild-mannered presenter who was the peacekeeper between the three antagonists. You would basically watch this program in the hope that it would all kick off between the agitants with the mild-mannered presenter losing complete control. He would then suffer in the ensuing chaos trying to restore order. Today it did not happen and my interest was diminishing rapidly. I decided to take a walk over to the playground stopping at the toilets at the back of the school building. The Victorian toilets at the back were very grand and ornate and attention to detail was everywhere. It was a monument and statement to civilized living with all the brass fittings polished and gleaming. The workmanship was precise and great pride had been taken in its construction. It was also not used much as it was off the beaten track and was very quiet. It was a great place to take a dump surrounded by all this splendour and opulence. As I was sitting there, I remembered a conversation I had with another student. He said that he used to save going to the toilet for as long as possible in order to attain the maximum feeling of relief when he jettisoned his payload. You do feel relieved, but I think he was taking it a bit too far. He was definitely weird and certainly a candidate for a dark dungeon full of fetish nerds. As soon as my load hit the water I was faced with the stark choice of very rough medicated toilet paper. If you have ever had the misfortune to use this, it is just like tracing paper and probably made in the same factory. You would need the undercarriage of a Sherman tank to use this stuff. After I had used just a few sheets, I was ready to throw in the towel with my anus waving a white flag clear and high. I finished up in the toilet and washed my hands. This was truly a gleaming palace of porcelain.

I made my way over to the playground and sat on one of the rope swings and began to swing away. I was a little old for swings and felt a bit awkward, but as soon as the rush and exhilaration hit me, I stopped caring. The school was situated on a hill with the main building to my left and a large church to my right. In front of me through the trees, I could see for miles. I was soaring back and forth with the swing jumping slightly on the high points. I had the feelings of elation and joy as I raced through the air with the wind coursing over me. This was great, things were going so well I had to pinch myself. I felt like the world was at my feet and it was all there for the taking if I wanted it. Joy was in my heart and I had turned a corner in my life. I was back on track. After a good time swinging, I returned to Robin Dorm common room. Everyone would be back soon and we would all be sitting down for lunch. I planned to see Sarah sometime after lunch and hopefully stay there until the evening. I was watching telly when everyone arrived back and I was greeted enthusiastically. It was handshakes and embraces all round and smiles were in abundance. I did miss them and in a way, I was happy to be back despite Sarah.

When you're the leader of a dorm, it's not like you can sit back and relax. You can't. There are real problems to deal with daily, and coming back after a long absence means the imaginary intray will be full of backed up shit that needs to be dealt with. Kirk was top of the list of troubles again and had been spanking the monkey with great energy and enthusiasm in my absence. Strong words would have to be used, but I think in reality, only a castration would solve his problem. There were other issues with money being borrowed and not paid back and it was all handed to me to resolve. I think the phrase rhymes with clucking bell.

After lunch, I made my way to the Sick Ward and was greeted by Matron.

"How are you young Paul," she said.

"Fine, thank you, Matron," I said.

Matron was in high spirits and escorted me over to Sarah's bed.

"Look who's here young beauty," Matron said.

Sarah was resting in an upright position. She opened her eyes and immediately uttered my name.

"Paul," she said.

She grasped me with both arms like she hadn't seen me for an eternity. Matron then made her excuses.

"I'll leave you two lovebirds alone," Matron said.

Sarah was overjoyed and her face was filled with happiness. As soon as Matron turned the corner at the end of the ward we were kissing urgently and with purpose. I was struggling to breathe with the sheer intensity of our passion. I was suffocating in ecstasy as our lips pressed and tongues encircled and stroked. Our hunger was immense as we devoured and consumed each other relentlessly. I became aroused very quickly and at this point, I just wanted to cast my clothes aside and take her, but I couldn't. We were not alone and Matron could appear at any time and get a nasty shock.

So we reluctantly slowed down and concluded. I pulled up a chair and laid my head next to her lap as she ran her fingers through my hair. It was still very intimate, but way more acceptable than banging Sarah in the middle of the day. Her hand moving over my head was very soothing, and it was making me feel very calm and thoughtful. I asked Sarah if she remembered the time I had detention in her dorm and did she know that I could see her.

"I knew, and my dance was for you, " she said. I went on to explain that it was the first time that I thought I might have a chance with her and it really lifted me.

"I wanted to speak to you, but you were gone the next day," she said.

She then told me how she missed me being around and that she had to do something to see me. Her plan was simple but effective. She got her friend Gabby to jump on her foot. I was astonished and amazed at the extent of her sacrifice just to see me. Her dedication was above and beyond any expectations and without it, we probably would not be where we are now. She had also kept it a secret and only now had divulged this minor detail. For me, it was a bombshell that engaged my mind. There really was no doubting her commitment.

"Did it hurt?" I said,

"Like crazy, but It was worth it," she said.

This was better than Romeo and Juliet. The courage to do something like that. She could have broken her foot easily and ended up in the local hospital. She had been fearless in her pursuit of me and I was very grateful. My admiration and respect for her were enormous and not just in my pants. We were the perfect match and I could not imagine life without her.

I stayed with my head by her side immersed in her adoration as her fingers ran lovingly through my hair. At this point, Matron came around on one of her visits and was surprisingly unphased by our activity.

"Will you be staying to eat Paul," Matron said.

I sat up away from Sarah's soothing fingers.

"Yes, if that's OK Matron. Thank you," I said.

Matron smiled warmly.

"Of course it's OK Paul. I'll get that organised,"
she said.

I was here for the evening without even having to ask.
My favourite TV show Star Trek was on today as well
and maybe Sarah would watch it with me. Once we had
eaten and were alone we made our way over to the sofa
with a blanket. The TV area was secluded and just off
the main ward. I turned the telly on and selected the
channel. Star Trek had not started yet and it was still
showing Mastermind, which would make most people
comatose and possibly dribble from one side of their
mouth. I returned to the sofa and snuggled up with
Sarah. She was so warm and so soft. How did I ever get
to be this lucky? As we sat there being lobotomised by
Magnus Magnuson, Sarah put her hand on it and said:

"I've started so I'll finish."

She then proceeded to dive under the cover and unzip me. No encouragement was needed as my swollen manhood jumped to attention. She then began to kiss, lick, suck, fondle and gobble, on my grateful penis. I would not be going on a journey with Magnus which would make my head hurt intensely. Instead, I would be running through a buttercup field with Sarah on a pleasure journey which would rock my senses and feed my soul. I barely noticed that Star Trek had already started as Sarah continued to deliver her magic. She had brought me close to the brink of ecstasy and now she would finish the job. Her pace quickened, rubbing faster and more vigorously, and when I heard Captain Kirk say:

"Warp speed, Scotty."

My senses overloaded and it was all too much as my hot white man jelly escaped at speed and I ejaculated all over Sarah. After a major cleanup operation involving countless tissues, we both emerged and returned to a more acceptable demeanour. We became two likeable endearing angels with absolutely no evidence of any wrongdoing.

Football (soccer) was my favourite game and we would play nearly every day, especially after school, when classes were finished. We had a floodlit football pitch with 5 a-side goals, but our numbers were always greater. With the lighting, we could play up till bedtime if we wanted and often did. All the regulars, including myself, were all good players and many of us were in the school team. We had a game coming up which we needed to prepare for and these guys from Shirley Green School were bastards and seriously dirty. They would go for your legs and not the ball and they wouldn't care if you left the pitch on a stretcher. This team was top of our league and they would always win ugly and at any cost. This would be our toughest game and we would have to adapt our play to combat the player assault. It was also a home game and with all our supporters, the advantage would be with us. We hoped.

On the day of the game, it was a bright sunny day with not a cloud in the sky. We had so many supporters, I couldn't even see if Sarah was here. As the whistle went the ball was played, and we were stroking it around with belief and resolve. After 2o minutes of play, we seemed to be in the ascendancy with most of the good early chances falling to us. But against the run of play, one of their players went down in instalments in the penalty box. The gullible referee swallowed the ruse like a fine red wine, giving a penalty for the theatrics. The ball was placed on the spot to the sound of whistles and jeers, but it made no difference as our hapless keeper was sent the wrong way. The ball was guided in, just inside the post. We were now behind and as the game continued their challenges became more physical and dangerous. One of their players known as the Ginger Assassin was responsible for the majority of the barbarous tackles. Our play was being gravely disrupted, and by half time we had lost two good players to injury. At the interval, we were in need of some managerial resurrection and a concrete battle plan. But our manager Mr Keating was not a man for the big moments, he was a modest man and not very inspiring. There would be no battle cry and the troops would not be fired up and mobilized. Besides, I already knew what I needed to do before he even spoke and it would not be pretty.

As we came out for the second half we knew we would have to stop the Ginger Assassin and score twice to win the game. They were attacking our goal early in the second half when they were awarded a corner. As the cross came over Ginger was right behind me and almost pushing me over with his physicality. With his close presence, the name of the game was to surprise. I was able to grab hold of his nuts and squeeze them to destruction as he screamed just like a little girl. To all those watching the game and the players on the pitch, my hand was hidden between us, and its exploits were not visible. Even the vigilant referee who had called some howlers in the game could not see any corruption of Ginger's credentials. When Ginger hit the ground he was writhing in agony with his hands between his legs. He remained in this state until he was carried off on a stretcher, with his final destination being the local hospital. More bad fortune was to follow when surgery that was intended to restore full function to Ginger's flattened beans, was botched by an inexperienced rookie surgeon. I discovered later that one of his testicles was removed with his remaining one barely functioning. It remained mainly for aesthetic purposes. The family jewels had been ransacked and were not in a great way. His chances of fathering a child were negligible and the pitter-patter of a tiny Ginger Assassin would sadly need a miracle of biblical proportions.

With Ginger tucked up in a hospital bed, the game would now start to turn in our direction and we started to create more and more chances. Their goal was leading a charmed life when eventually, we made the long-awaited breakthrough. A speculative effort from outside the box which dipped over their keeper clipping the bar on the way in. It was Beefy Brightwell who celebrated by taking his boot off and making it look like he was taking a phone call before he was mobbed. We were level. They were still trying to chop us down but without Ginger, they couldn't knock the fluff off a cappuccino. It was near to the end and we were still deadlocked. We would feel aggrieved if we didn't win this one. The game was entering its final moments and we had just won a corner. As the ball came over I could see it was flighted perfectly. I rose in front of the defender just inside the box with the near post to my left. As the ball made contact with my forehead I twisted my head to the left and guided the ball towards the goal. The ball arced over the keeper who was at full stretch trying to reach it. I then watched the ball dip just under the crossbar in the far corner. We were ahead and we absolutely deserved it. I punched the air with excitement but before I could celebrate properly, I was pinned to the ground with everyone piling in on top of me. They were all screaming crazily with joy and amazement at what they had just witnessed. Football, fucking hell. This was a wild, fantastic, remarkable, lump in your throat moment. When the final whistle blew we all fell to our knees, we even had a mini-pitch invasion with all our supporters and classmates sensing that this was something very special. All the players were being patted, hugged, congratulated and helped back to their feet. Even our Headmaster who not that long ago was giving me six of the best was eager to greet me.

"Brilliant goal Paul, just brilliant," he said as he patted me on the back.

"Thank you, Sir. I just got lucky," I said.
We both smiled excitedly, carried away by the euphoria of the moment. As we parted I could see Sarah with her friend Gabby making their way over with beaming smiles and I greeted them both with a big hug. I didn't know Gabby that well and we had only just started acknowledging each other. She was Sarah's

best friend and from what she had told me about her, I knew she was good, loyal and the keeper of all Sarah's secrets. She probably knew about every encounter between us.

"Paul, You look so sexy in your football kit," Sarah said smiling.

"I'm saving it all for you," I said with a wink.

Sarah and Gabby were whispering and when they had finished Gabby said that she had to go. She then said goodbye and left us alone. I don't know what came over me, but I spontaneously decided that I needed to get away from all the celebration and noise. I wanted to be alone with Sarah

"Do you have money? If you do, let's go to the burger bar," I said.

"A little, not a great deal," She said

"Let's do it, let's escape for a while," I said with a cheeky smile.

I took her by the hand holding it tightly. I kind of knew she would follow me almost anywhere, apart from a burning pit of flames maybe. I strolled towards the woods, leading her through the narrow pathways. At the back of the woods, there was a gap in the large wire fence. We navigated through the gap and down a dirt track which led to the main road. We were free and it was a wonderful feeling to escape your confines. We were breaking the rules again, but as the hero of the day, I think I had accumulated a little grace. I was still in my kit, but I really didn't care. The burger bar was within sight and in a small parade of shops. When we arrived, we sat and looked at the menu. Sarah carefully pulled out her loose change which only gave us enough for one burger and chips and one soft drink.

"It's OK, we will share," I said.

"Sorry, at least we have something," she said.
I held both her hands across the small table as the waitress came over to take our order. We were the only ones there apart from an old couple on the far side. Sarah gave her order and paid the money upfront with her loose change and the waitress went away. She

squeezed my hands and smiled, then we both leaned in and kissed.

"Do you feel OK about being here and bunking school," I said.

"I feel great, you've got me breaking all the rules again," she laughed

"I just wanted us to have some time, I really miss being alone with you," I said.

"Me-too, I think about it all the time, Even in lessons, and I can't concentrate," she said.

"If we can get away with this, maybe we can get away with other things," I said.

"Your right, we will find times and places to be together," she said.

Sarah stood up and sat beside me and put her head on my shoulder, Then she snuggled up. She felt good pressed against me.

"Did you know that Gabby likes that strange friend of yours...Kirk," she said

Strange was damn right and there really was no accounting for taste. Kirk was like a child in a big hairy man's body and was probably born as a giant hairball. He looked way ahead of his years and could certainly walk into a pub unchallenged and order a pint. His chest was like a dense rainforest and he had hands like shovels. If he had a brain he would be dangerous. He was also awkward around most people and nearly always said the wrong thing. But I didn't dislike Kirk and he did have a good side that not many people would see. This information was dynamite, maybe we could fix them up. He might change his ways if he had a girlfriend. He deserved a chance and perhaps I could help him. It may even stop all the cover pounding that went on at night and keep the sanity of his already fragile bed neighbours.

"Stop the world I want to get off. I would never have guessed that," I said.

"It's true, she talks about him all the time," she said.

"Gabby helped to get us together so I think we should help her to meet Kirk," I said.

"Hey, that's a great idea. You could set it up and I could let her know," she said.

We were then interrupted by the waitress serving our order. They must have taken pity on us as they served a very large portion of fries as if they knew we wanted more but didn't have the money. We both thanked the waitress as the smell of fries and burger filled the air. I was very hungry after running around a field for 90 minutes, but I wanted Sarah to enjoy her time here so I held back. She held the burger to her lips and bit daintily into the soft sesame seed bun. She could have been in a burger commercial with her golden hair catching the sun. I had become an onlooker to a virtuoso performance and was salivating just watching her. After two more teasing, tantalising bites, she offered up the burger to my hungry mouth. That plump juicy succulent burger was just begging to be devoured mercilessly and it took all of my willpower to take a single pathetic bite. If it were just me and that burger locked in a cage the struggle would be over very quickly with me sitting there content with a full stomach.

"Take some more," she said.

I took another bite. This sure was a tasty burger and being so hungry made it twice as nice. She pressed the burger to my mouth like she was feeding a child that wouldn't eat and as I gulped down my mouth opened for another burger fill up. After I took another bite I could see the burger was depleted and down to a single bite. As I chewed I pushed the last bite back to Sarah who gratefully scoffed it down. I liked being fed and it was another example of what we couldn't do back at the school. The fries homed into view and I took a few and started feeding Sarah, placing them one by one in her open mouth. Sarah reciprocated and I too was being fed with love and fries. When we finished all the fries we were full and ready for the cold drink to wash it down with. Sarah didn't wait and the cold refreshing beverage was emptying quickly. There was no need to worry as the drink was duly held in front of me and the straw pressed between my lips. I didn't realise how thirsty I was as the gloriously cold sweet concoction filled my mouth and flowed down my throat. Sadly It ran out all too quickly but it was enough to keep me going for now. The food and drink were finished, but Sarah wanted to play. She took the plastic lid of the paper drink cup and pulled a cube of ice out. I was puzzled as she told me to stay still and close my eyes. I trusted her completely so I went along with her and shut my eyes. I then felt the ice slowly run over my lips. Then over my eyes and my eyebrows, then around my cheeks and my chin. A tranquil peace came over me as the long day started to catch up. I sat there motionless as the ice travelled up and down the contours of my face again and again. I was so relaxed and soothed that I started to tingle all over as I got goose pimples. I was now in a daydream state with all my cares and inhibitions just sliding away. As the ice gradually melted a paper tissue was used to gently pat and dry my face. I then felt her lips against mine, softly caressing them back to life as all my senses returned. Just like that, she had switched me back on again.

We were living in liberal times indeed, for sure, as the next bombshell to hit me was revealed by Sarah on our walk back to the school. Apparently, she had asked Matron if she could go on the pill before she even came to the sick ward, and Matron had agreed. She got the idea after a sex education class where they were told to see Matron prior to any sexual activity. They really were covering their arses in this place with the tablets being handed out like candy. When you have lots of young people with their hormones running wild and out of control, things are definitely going to happen. They must have found out over the years that it is better to prevent than leave the door open to unwanted pregnancies. Daughters going home with big bellies would not exactly be on the school curriculum or in the glossy school brochure which glorified educational achievement and excellence. Fine school establishments do not send their young ladies home with flushed cheeks and a bun in the oven. They position themselves on the moral high ground that the parents demand and do not sanction any corruption of their young ladies. So, just to recap, they don't condone any sexual activity whatsoever, but there is contraception available for those that want to bend and manipulate the rules a little. It sounds to me like a green light for everyone to get busy shagging and throw all caution and restraint to the wind. Don't just watch those heaving breasts and bouncing buttocks, get stuck in and indulge yourself. Your sexual frustrations will be at an end as you can shag away in the reassuring knowledge that everyone is on the pill. There would definitely be no comebacks whatsoever in this alluring cherry poppers safe haven. I looked at Sarah in disbelief. I knew she was being sensible, but how did she know she was going to need it.

"Why are you looking at me like that," she said.

"I wasn't even with you when you asked for the pill," I said.

"I know, but I planned to be with you and now I am. So what's wrong," she said.

I thought about her perfect answer. It did seem a bit clinical and calculating, but she was with me and there was no doubting her love and commitment. Besides, I couldn't think of a damn thing to say in return, so I just said:

"Your right, nothing is wrong."

We stopped in the woods on the way back. There was a large fallen tree which lay along the ground at just below waist height. Sarah laid over it with her bum sticking up as I pulled her knickers down and held her dress up. This is what she had signed up for when she started taking the pill and I wasn't going to disappoint. For me, there has always been something very arousing about taking a woman from behind. A woman's bum takes on a whole new erotic shape when it is pushed out into the air and it just screams, insert your cock here. My penis pushed its way between her wet lips and plunged deep inside her as her moaning became much louder than I was comfortable with. I put her hand over her mouth and the noise subsided as I thrust and pressed harder against her swollen pussy. I was holding her waist with my hands as her body started convulsing and she gripped my wrist very tightly. Her breathing was hard as she shrieked and moaned heavily. Her perfectly formed bum and the way it was moving was pushing my excitement levels into the red zone, as I felt my testicles tighten and then release repeatedly. I stayed there for a while teasing her with my presence, but eventually, we had to go as we would be missed. As we got to the main building, I told Sarah to go on ahead as it would look suspicious if we turned up together. We kissed, then she ran towards the door. The day had been so full, I would sleep like a baby all night.

Breakfast time was the same every day with a full fried English breakfast, cereal if you wanted, grapefruit in juice, mandarins in juice, tea, coffee, fruit juices, milk, toast, butter, and jams. At breakfast, we would always sit at the same hexagon-shaped table and in the same seat. Lunch was a little different with many more people sitting to eat, so more tables with self-service. At my table (breakfast and dinner) sat my Housemaster Bill, myself, Beefy, Simon, Kirk, Kevin, all from my dorm. Bill was probably somewhere in his 50's and was born with a deformity in one leg, which was also shorter and weaker than his good leg. To compensate for this, he had to wear a big clumpy boot which evened him up and supported his lower leg where it was weak. The boot had metal rods going to knee supports which strapped above and below the knee. There was also a clicking contraption on both sides of his boot which clicked over and back with each stride that he took. Bill looked like he had just jumped out of the 1930s. He always had short back and sides, well-kept moustache, wore skinny ties, skinny shirt collars and drainpipe trousers. Whenever we were misbehaving his clicking boot was literally his Achilles heel as it alerted us to his presence long before he arrived. It was like our early warning system. Bill was a good Housemaster and had been at Outwood since God was a small boy. Over the few years, I had known Bill I had come to respect him and see him as a father figure. He was always there with advice and you could see it wasn't just a job for him. He got involved and he worked with us. He was on our side as long as we didn't go overboard. He was one of the team apart from the few times when he would have to do his job. He then became a little officious to show that he was in charge.

School assembly was held on weekdays normally half an hour after breakfast. On the weekends we had no assembly and were allowed to wear casual clothes which we all prefered over wearing school uniform. One day we were all gathered for assembly and it seemed like just another day at the office. The Headmaster had made a call for uniforms to be worn properly at all times with no loose ties, rolled up sleeves, dresses just above the knees and not any higher. There was a trend at the school that was taking the girls dresses higher up the thighs. If one of these girls bent over near you, two firm perfectly formed rounded buttocks would peekaboo into view and really leave nothing to the imagination. The last time this happened to me I took my frustrations out on Sarah and smashed her back doors in. I was a little embarrassed after but she seemed to enjoy it which made me feel less guilty. When the Headmaster stopped speaking he gave way to another teacher who took up the reins. Now it was about the litter problem in the school. My god, they were literally making minuscule problems sound like major catastrophes. Litter would always get cleared away with the army of after school cleaners and the janitor. None of this was mentioned. Why did we have to sit through this shit? As I sat there losing the will to live something out of the ordinary happened. One of the senior girls jumped up on the stage and started to accuse the Headmaster of having a sexual relationship with her to everyone's gasps of amazement. This could have been dismissed if it wasn't for the tears in her eyes and the emotion in her voice. We were all left in no doubt that this indeed was the case and the Headmaster who was a family man with 2 young children of his own had been pumping one of the 6th formers (12th grade) on the quiet. Probably by spanking her bare buttocks before he started. Sorry, it's a power dominance thing. We all sat there gobsmacked with the silence compounding the agony for the accused, who was slowly turning a brighter shade of red. Finally, two teachers reluctantly summoned up the courage to escort the young lady away. They had to physically restrain her as they passed the now-disgraced Headmaster who was definitely looking very sheepish, out of steam and without a paddle. The teachers all pulled together like a threatened regime and rallied around their wounded leader. The incident as convincing as it was would not be taken seriously and would not leave the confines of the school. No higher authority would hear of this matter and the case was covered over and closed. These days he would have been crucified at the stake with his nuts removed for good measure and placed on the altar of moral virtue. But back then it was an indiscretion that could be survived. Sure some of the mud would stick, but time is a great healer and memories fade. Down the line, he would find it hard making speeches on righteousness, decency, and being trustworthy. But these were his problems and he alone would have to come to terms with them. I was relieved in a way as I had got to know Headmaster, who had mostly been on my side on many matters that ended up in his office. He was responsible in some part in helping me banish Big Bull to the pit of despair from which he would never return. Yes, I was glad he survived. He had assisted me in the past and may yet do so again.

A school trip was coming up to the Isle of Wight and I really didn't want to go. It was organised by a teacher called Maurice that used to be a monk back in the day and was now somewhere between a back to nature man and a hippy. The trip would be for the whole of my dorm for the whole weekend with a coach taking us there and back. Normally I would have jumped at the opportunity to get away but now I was with Sarah, I didn't want to be anywhere else but here with her. There was no choice though, I was on the list and nothing short of the meltdown of society would prevent me from going. I was up all night thinking about it, the best I could come up with was to get Gabby the disabler to jump on my foot. It wouldn't take Colombo to work out a recurring injury in the Sick Ward. Hey-ho, I would just have to bite the bullet and go. Maybe it would surprise me and be a good trip. I had never been to the Isle of Wight before. I would keep an open mind. Sarah and I would miss each other for sure, but absence makes the heart grow fonder.

Orange Chapter

The coach left the school an hour after last class on
Friday evening and everyone was in good spirits.
Maurice was the leader with Bill filling in as assistant
at the last moment. We would be taking a ferry in
Southampton with the coach to Cowes. When we
arrived it was still daylight and there would be a
half-hour wait for the ferry to load and depart. We were
waiting in a line for coaches and trucks when we all got
out to stretch our legs. Everything seemed a little
unorganised as some of us went to the shops over the

way, some stayed and some went to the back of the coach for a crafty fag (cigarette). Maurice decided to go over to the shops and keep an eye on that group while Bill stayed behind with the main group. There were large plumes of smoke rising from the back of the coach as the smoking party got into full swing. The smokers were taking advantage of the laxity and exploiting it. I nearly said to Bill that there was an engine fire, but I didn't want to appear like I was poking fun at the situation, so I just kept quiet. After a while, the lines started to move and we were all told to board the coach. After chasing up the stragglers and the never on time brigade, we eventually started moving towards the ferry. As we got underway, packed lunches were handed out to all of us for the trip over to Cowes. Our coach drove down a large gantry into the ferry and parked up behind another coach, we then disembarked our vehicle. We followed Maurice up a wide stairway which led to a large dining area, seating area and observation deck. All of us sat by the windows so we had a really good view. For most of us, it was our first time on a boat and we wanted to experience it to the full. The sandwiches were great, turkey and stuffing and egg mayonnaise , all made by the school kitchen staff. The comedian of our group, Simon, was not feeling too good after the long coach ride. So, we helped ourselves to his free sandwiches, oblivious to the suffering that he was enduring. Soon the ferry started moving as we all shouted in unison:

"More power Scotty."

Simon was not looking good as the ferry reached warp factor one on its tired engines. His pale complexion and lacklustre demeanour were getting Bill and Maurice concerned. He was given a plastic bag and told to use it if he was sick as the sympathy subsided and ebbed away. Not long after, Simon was retching and heaving into the empty bag, filling it close to capacity. A delicate operation was required to remove the offending bag which was not exactly watertight.

Maurice looked at Bill and vice-versa, it was decided that Maurice would deal with it, as there was dripping in one corner. He was the only one with two good legs which made Maurice the automatic choice for the job. Quick's the word and sharp's the action, was needed in this daring game of hold on tight and don't let the bag break. The only way out was through the dining area which was full of happy eaters. He made his way through with his pace quickening on the path of doom or glory. His confidence grew as he closed in on the doors out to the deck, but the flimsy bag conspired against him and weakened. It ripped open under the strain and the contents gushed out like an unstoppable tide as the noxious smell permeated the air all around. Maurice looked down to see the floor covered all around him, it was game over. Time to look down, be solemn, don't make eye contact at all and avoid at all costs, the angry mob, with a swift exit. Later that evening back at the hotel, Maurice could see the funny side of it, as we all made jokes about the sick bag bomber, which soon became his nickname. We finished the day with a slap-up fish and chips meal in the hotel and even Simon was well enough to eat again.

The hotel was excellent and very large. I thought we would be in some budget place, but not at all, it was really impressive. There were three of us to each room, so with Maurice and Bill having separate rooms, we had 12 rooms altogether. Perhaps they got some special rate for a large booking. With so many rooms they would not be able to watch them all, they would even have to knock to get entry. It was a licence for the opportunists amongst us to misbehave. There was also some big event taking place downstairs and when the music started playing we knew it was a party. I was sharing my room with Beefy and Kirk. Beefy was a small blonde Viking genius, who was slight in stature. He was called beefy because he wasn't. He was very articulate and knew all the big words. He was also very good at football which made him fit right in. Beefy was a great conversationalist and could talk rings around people on most subjects. As the music continued we went on a reconnaissance trip to see what was going on. We found out just by standing at the top of the stairs that it was a fancy dress party that seemed to be open to all comers. The three of us returned to our room and after a very short discussion, we all decided to go for it. If we were discovered we could be banned from future school trips which was not much of a concern as I tried to get out of this one. As it was a fancy dress, we would all go in our pyjamas and slippers and wear underpants on our heads just to get in the party mood. As we arrived, we immediately recognised that all the drinks were free. With punch bowls strategically placed all around the large function hall. We gathered around one of the punch bowls, like thirsty wildebeest at a watering hole and we started to indulge ourselves. Everyone around us was under the influence or completely hammered. It was like we were wearing invisible cloaks and were wandering around unseen. We found some comfy seats and sat down, with the drink starting to make us all smile. After an unknown number of trips to the punch bowls, we started talking complete gibberish and we were loving it. We were bouncing silly ideas off one another which made no sense to anyone but the drunk. We all jabbered and muttered regardless of anyone paying attention or not, in one soliloquy after another. I started to notice a young lady and every time I looked up she was looking right back at me. She had a figure to die for with beautiful rounded stand-alone breasts. She was blonde and I had a weakness for blondes even if they were fake. I was stupid like that with my primitive urges overriding my fully developed functioning brain. The music was starting to become infectious as we all got up and removed our head underwear. We all made our way to the dancefloor and started to move with the beat. Beefy and I were dancing well, but Kirk was off tempo and his dancing was untidy and chaotic with no rhythm. The beat had eluded him and he was irregular and out of sync. But I really admired his commitment and unity. He was getting involved and joining in and not sitting it out with a note from Matron. He was one of us and as such, was deserving of our respect. We had danced through a few songs when I suddenly felt like another drink. I gestured with my hand that I was going for another drink, and it all felt a little slow and not quite right. They were both a little wasted themselves but looked happy and I was glad we got to do this. As I approached the punchbowl I could see the young lady who was eyeballing me earlier and she was extensively easy on the eyes. As I filled my glass and turned my head she was there:

"Hello, I'm Eleanor," she said.

"Hi, I'm Paul," I said.

"Pleased to meet you, Paul," she said.

Her smell was divine like I was strolling through a rose garden in full bloom. I had never been around a female that stimulated my nose so much. It was such a sweet bouquet of fragrant aromas and I was instantly drawn to her. I was starting to think the unthinkable as a red hot carnival was taking place in my pants. I was beginning to get aroused.

"You smell really good," I said.

"Thank you, do you puff. I have some weed in my room," she said.

"Sure, why not," I said.

This was great. I had smoked many times, mainly socially but weed was like the Holy Grail and I was about to partake. We had all joked about being stoned at our smoking parties, but this was the real deal and a big milestone in my life. She led the way to the elevator and I followed. We were both slightly merry and comfortable in our bubbles. As we took the elevator, We started studying each other in a casual relaxed way. We were both smiling as I began to wonder if there would be more on offer than the weed and the possibilities were getting me excited. I needed some weed to calm me down. When we got to her room, she made herself comfortable on the sofa and patted the seat next to her for me to sit there. I duly obliged. She had all the goodies on her coffee table and I sat and watched in awe as she carefully rolled a very large joint.

"Do you want to go first," she said.

"OK," I said.

She lit the joint and puffed until it was burning freely. It was then presented to me. I held it in my fingers with admiration and slowly took my first tug and drew the smoke down. I tried so hard not to cough, but the smoke was so thick and pungent that I couldn't help it. She laughed.

"Here let me help you," she said.

I gave her the burning joint and she took a tug.

"Open your mouth," she said.

She took a larger tug and moved her mouth towards mine. Her mouth then covered mine as she released the smoke into my lungs. After she had administered a few more shotgun kisses, I began to feel very calm and relaxed. It was a great way to break the ice, as we soon began exploring each other's bodies as our clothes fell away. I was feeling slightly tranquilised. I was there but slightly withdrawn and restful from my usual self. I laid back on the sofa as my cock stood up in the air like a flag pole. Eleanor climbed aboard as she rode my cock to destruction. She was making so much noise and screaming so loudly in parts, that I thought there would be a knock on the door. When she screamed she would grip my body tightly, digging me with her long nails. At some point, she stopped and started licking my dick and paying a little attention to my balls. My flagpole was still in the air as she mounted it once again. She rode harder this time and with more vigour and it wasn't long before her nails were pressing deep into my skin as her screams echoed around the room. Eleanor really had an appetite and she was determined to drain my nuts at any cost. She stopped for a while and kissed me on the lips for the first time. Then she went again, grinding harder than ever and making my cock push deeper. Her body tightened and her nails dug hard into my skin once again. She was screaming louder than ever as I felt my balls tense up and shoot their great load over and over. Eleanor felt it too and became very vocal:

"Oh my god, just like that, yes, yes, yes, yes," she said.

She stayed on me for some time draining every last drop from my depleted sacks.

I staggered out of Eleanor's room in the early hours and I had to ask myself, who was I and where was I, as my brain was slow to engage. Then I remembered Beefy and Kirk and the room number was 222 which was easy to recall even in my fragile state. When I got to the door, someone had wedged a sock in the door frame to stop it from closing. Beefy was way too clever and destined for higher things. I opened the door to the sound of deep slumber. My bed was beckoning me to immerse myself in its warm enveloping softness. I collapsed into it and went out like a light. I barely enjoyed my sleep as the morning arrived all too quickly and I was not in a good way, in fact, I felt awful. I lingered in bed until the last possible moment, before rising with a very sore head. I made it down to the buffet breakfast with everyone looking so refreshed and alive. My energy and alertness though were lacking and far below my normal self, I made some tea, ate some toast and I started to feel a little better until I heard some talk about a screaming lady. I kept my head low and told myself not to worry. Nobody could possibly know I was involved, except maybe Beefy or Kirk. Thank god she wasn't screaming my name, that would narrow the field down considerably. Then, it would only be a matter of time before the accusing finger was pointed at me. I looked up at Beefy and Kirk, who were both smiling back at me and I realized instantly that they knew. An enormous dread feeling overcame me as my moral lapse was no longer a secret. I was a useless article with an inability to control my actions, I had so much already to be good for. I had let myself and Sarah down so badly and I was overflowing with guilt. I hated myself and I would never let this happen again. My philandering although good at the time was now causing me deep anxiety. I wasn't someone who could deal with multiple relationships and if it got back to Sarah, she would finish with me and I would totally deserve it. She was everything to me and I really didn't want to break up with her. What I had done was amusement without any feelings. I was flattered that I could get someone older, but Eleanor, the drink, the weed and the availability of all were a deadly combination. It may well come back with a terrible bite.

After breakfast when we went back to our room, I spoke to Beefy and Kirk and laid all the cards on the table. I told them how much I loved Sarah and that I couldn't bear to lose her. What I had done was a big mistake and I regretted it completely. I told them about my overwhelming fears that Sarah would leave me and I could see in their faces that they knew I was sincere. They immediately agreed it should go no further. We had a bond of trust and it made us closer as friends. I also told Kirk he had a secret admirer and that I wanted to set up a date, and when I told him who it was, he looked very happy. I now felt a bit more upbeat as we continued getting ready for Osborne House. The coach was waiting when we made it to the front of the hotel. It would be a short journey from Ryde to East Cowes.

Osborne House was Queen Victoria's favourite getaway residence and life here was without the stresses of court life. It was very grand in size and style, I just wished I could enjoy it more. We had a guide who was very knowledgeable, but I was having trouble keeping up with him in my weakened state. The sandman was shutting me down bit by bit as my eyes started to droop and my body began to ache. I needed to sleep but where? I remembered a few rooms back, there was a no entry sign on one of the doors. I told Simon I needed the toilet and backtracked down the corridor and found the sign. I opened the door and found it was just another room, but more importantly, it was a bedroom with a large four-poster bed. I closed the door, took my shoes off and climbed into it. It was very comfy, and so it should be, Queen Victoria herself may have slept here, it could even be her deathbed. The sheets were smelly, musty and old, but I was too tired to care. I was soon dreaming about Sarah and I was telling her how much I loved her and cared for her. The dream though started to turn bad. Eleanor appeared naked with a giant spliff and started chasing me as I ran from her, just like a Benny Hill sketch. She caught me and forced me with her erotic suggestiveness to smoke the giant smouldering bud. We were in the beautiful Garden of Eden and the Serpent was waiting for a tug on the hazardous joint. The more I smoked the more my penis got aroused and the more Eleanor licked her lips in anticipation. She had a smile hinting of mischief. Suddenly she was astride, riding me hard as the Serpent puffed on the joint of oblivion with its eyes looking glazed and vacant. But just behind the serpent was the Tree of Knowledge and Sarah was standing there crying and sobbing as she looked upon my excess debauchery with Eleanor in disbelief. I had the frailties of man, I was weak, I had destroyed the one thing that meant so much to me. Eleanor started laughing as I involuntarily ejaculated. Could things get any lower? I pushed Eleanor aside and made my way over to Sarah and held my hand out, but she moved away. What she had seen had deeply affected her and I wasn't surprised. I had been rejected and there was only one thing for it. I walked towards the tree of knowledge and started to climb it until I reached the very top. It was all over for us and I knew it could never be recovered. My tears were cascading down my cheeks over my loss and I just wanted the torment to end. I stood on the highest branch feeling the pain of rejection and the loss of my true love. It was all over. I fell through the air gaining speed with the ground closed in quickly. When I hit terra firma I woke up with a jolt. I had a cold sweat but I was still alive. That was the most awful, dark, vivid dream, I had ever had, with the whole thing feeling so real and emotional. A psychologist could probably decipher a lot of meaning out of such a dream. For instance, dreams with nudity can mean vulnerability, falling uncontrollably from a great height can mean things are out of your control. Death, you would expect to be perceived as negative, but no, it often signifies a dramatic change for the dreamer. One thing I knew for sure, was that this whole situation was consuming my mind to the point of having dreams about it. I looked around at all the Victorian grandeur and highly elaborate decorative features, what they built and achieved was extraordinary. I got out of the bed and made the covers up again, nobody would ever know. I was now refreshed and ready to take on the world. There was a musty smell and it had transferred from the bed to my clothes, I would just have to accept it. I found a mirror and my hair was sticking up, but there was no water, so saliva would have to do. I started wetting my hair down, preening and after tucking my shirt in I was looking alive again. I went over to the window and I could see our guide with our group following. I made a dash for the door and ran down the corridor and on to the gardens. As I caught them up I tagged onto the back of the line, as if I had been there all along. We had finished the garden tour and were making our way down to the private sandy beach where Queen Victoria would use her bathing machine. For those of you that are in the dark, a bathing machine was a walled wooden cart with a roof which rolled into the sea. It normally had curtains at each end which would allow the occupant entry and access to the sea after changing. Some would even have toilets built-in. These carts were part of social etiquette and rigorously enforced on women especially. The bathing suits women wore were extremely modest by today's standards, but they were still not meant to be seen or gazed upon when wearing them. How times have changed. For me, this was the standout part of the day and also the only part that I was involved in. The secret sleep remained secret as I was not missed. I was the vile dust, unwept, unhonoured and unsung, at least I hope not.

Sepia Chapter

After a leisurely day at Osborne House, Sleeping in Queen Victoria's bed and taking in some of the attractions, I was on a roll, but I had missed out on the packed lunch meal and was kind of disappointed that it wasn't flagged up. I understood that this was also a day out for Bill and Maurice and they couldn't be vigilant all the time. They did have 30 scallywags to watch, all of whom were pulling in different directions of interest. Controlling us was hard, but blimey, Stevie Wonder with a three-legged guide dog could have done a better job. We all started to board the bus for the trip back to the hotel and it wasn't long before we were underway. I was Hank Marvin (starving) and my stomach was growling, I needed some sustenance quickly. Luckily Simon was being suggestive with a banana to all the passing motorists. He even at one point had the banana between his legs pressing it against the coach window, which was getting a lot of laughs. Bill and Maurice were looking like they were ready to swing into action, so I took the initiative and swooped on the banana, like a bird of prey. As Bill and Maurice came up the aisle, I quickly unpeeled and consumed it briskly. Wow, that really filled a hole and gave us all some fun on the way.

We arrived back at the hotel late afternoonish and after a speedy cleanup in our room, Me, Kirk and Beefy were back in the lobby area enjoying the leather seating and looking pretty. We were kings of all we surveyed with our lives just beginning and our futures looking bright, rosy and full of promise. As we sat there I noticed Eleanor by the elevator, and I made a beeline for her. The elevator doors opened just as I got there. Eleanor went in still not knowing I was behind her as I followed her in. It was only when she turned to face the doors that she clocked me.

"Hey Paul, how are you," she said pressing the button.

"I'm OK, I wanted to speak to you," I said.

"Sure, are you OK," she said.

"Yes and no," I said.

"We can talk in my room," she said.

The elevator doors opened and we walked a few doors down the corridor and arrived at her room. As we entered, we walked over to the sofa of recent pleasures. I had a stiffy just thinking about it, but I had to prove that I could be strong and banish those primitive needs and let the big brain do the thinking. Tonight Sarah will be proud of me and she will not be crying under the Tree of Knowledge.

"So, what did you want to tell me," she said.

She took off her top and revealed her bosom which was stretching her blouse to the limit. They were like two puppies straining at the leash with the possibility of escape tantalizingly close. I felt weak and vulnerable to her evocative display. She was exquisite and her breasts were in the top drawer of perfection. Despite the distractions, I started to speak and tell her what was on my mind. I went on to explain that I kinda regretted going with her and it wasn't because of her. I told her that she was great and even though I was a little drunk and stoned, I really enjoyed it with her. The problem was, I shouldn't have been doing it with anyone. Then I told her that I had a girlfriend called Sarah who I loved and how much guilt I was feeling over what I had done. When I finished speaking I felt like a great burden had been lifted and I was free from its shackles. I was still guilty, but I was making a huge effort not to repeat the offence and in the face of the gift of her desirable body. If I couldn't be loyal to the one I love, then I just wasn't good enough for Sarah and eventually, my own guilt would consume me. This is because people always think that others behave and think the same way they do. If somebody is unfaithful, they will assume others close to them are unfaithful also, because they themselves are that way. It's just human bloody nature. The only way to break this cycle is to be the best you can be. Don't have affairs, be loyal and don't be suspicious of others. Just concentrate on yourself, because everything else is out of your control. A clear conscience is a fantastic thing and will liberate you in many ways. I really wanted to be a person that had one.

"Wow, Paul. That's so sweet that you care about her," Eleanor said.

"I know that I messed up, but I am trying to do the right thing now," I said.

"I understand, if you love her then you're right," Eleanor said.

"Thanks, I feel a bit sorry for you though," I said.

"Well, I have one more night, we can still do something as friends," Eleanor said.

"Yes definitely, I'll be free about 7.30," I said.

"OK, meet me here then and we can take a spin somewhere in my car," Eleanor said.

I left in a very good frame of mind having made my position very clear. She was quite special herself and had been very understanding with me. I did feel I had let her down slightly and it was niggling me some, but it was Sarah who I loved and she had to be told. I returned back to Kirk and Beefy in the relaxed atmosphere of mood music and extremely agreeable leather seating. I told them I was going out with Eleanor later but just as friends and I needed them to cover for me, which they both agreed to. I also said that I needed some money looking directly at Beefy. I looked at Beefy because he always had money and his family were extremely rich, which pretty much made him minted as well. He told me he had a fiver which he pushed into my open hand. I told him I would do my best to get him some weed. His eyes lit up like a fairground attraction. Nobody had offered him weed before and the possibility of obtaining something so inaccessible and out of reach was making him giddy. If I managed to obtain even a small amount, Beefy would be as happy as a dog with two tails. I could hear Bill's clicking boot as he entered the lobby area. We were then spotted as he made his way over to our leather sanctuary.

"Everybody OK," Bill said.

"Yes Bill," we all said.

"What was Simon up to earlier, " Bill said.

We all looked at each other. We were all aware of his exploits but really didn't want to blab on him, so I decided to speak knowing that Bill would accept my explanation.

"Sir we didn't take much notice of him. Simon is a bit weird and we do our best to avoid him," I said.

Simon was weird, but he was also very funny at times. He had provided us with most of the standout moments on the trip and the sick bag escapade was legendary.

We all had a sneaking admiration for Simon and none of us would want to see him up for the high jump.

"OK, that's fine, It's just the coach company had a complaint from someone saying there was rude behaviour onboard," Bill said.

It seems killjoys are everywhere, even on the Isle of Wight. These pompous, self-righteous, wouldn't piss in the bath, pruners of happiness, really get on my tits. Excuse my English. They will spend their lives worrying about what other people are doing, only to realise that their own life has passed them by without living it.

"No sir, we didn't see anything rude," I said with Kirk and Beefy agreeing.

"OK, dinner is at six.and we are eating here in the hotel, so let everyone know," Bill said.

Bill then walked away with the clicking boot fading as the distance between us increased. We were all busy thinking our own thoughts as we slouched on the chairs. I was thinking about my trip with Eleanor later.

Kirk was probably thinking about Gabby and Beefy was more than likely rolling a heavenly joint in his head with my promised weed. We were all relaxed and thoughtful and in a period of reflection and self-absorption. Simon somehow managed to make his way under our radar and immediately it was all over for us, as the magic was broken. The cheeky chappy filled the air with verbal nonsense, which none of us was too impressed with. He was a wannabe comic who desperately needed new material to invigorate his tired lines. He was not making any impression on us as we all grew weary, but he wasn't going to leave without making his mark. Simon was someone who would always end up surprising you, one way or another. He made himself comfortable and was just sitting there with a big mischievous smile on his face with a vacant expression as we all looked at him. He made no eye contact as his smile got wider. Why was he just sitting there smiling? We were bewildered at his inexplicable behaviour. Was he up to some monkey business or was he genuinely filled with happiness? Simon's face screamed mischief as he suddenly and without warning let rip with a massive fart blowout, which was so nasty and rotten you could taste it. We were all suffocating as it hung thick in the air around us. It was such an awful stench that it must have burnt his arse as he released it. After wafting more in our direction as if we needed a second helping, Simon ran off laughing as our bad language and curses followed him. Our sanctuary was now a no go zone as we all fled the carnage that had been wreaked upon us, in search of fresh air and respiratory assistance. Our sanctuary was now Ground Zero.

After dinner, we found a quiet corner for Simon where swift justice was administered. He had crossed the line and now he became the punchbag of our frustrations. We were gentle but firm as the blows were distributed over his body humanely. When we had finished we helped him back to his feet and brushed him off. He had survived his punishment in good shape and even managed a plucky smile as if to say, is that the best you can do. We had no desire to hurt Simon, it was just a little squeeze to say not on our doorstep ever again. We returned to our room leaving Simon to ponder his indiscretion. I still had half an hour to get ready and to rearrange with Eleanor to meet her in the hotel car park, which I managed to do. After all, I couldn't be seen leaving the hotel, especially not with a hot blonde. When the time came I made my way through the hotel unnoticed wearing Beefy's prized sunglasses and out of a side door into the car park. As I looked up, an impressive, shiny silver car pulled up beside me and the window went down.

"Get in Paul," Eleanor said.

"Hey, this is swank," I said.

She gave a confident smile as if she was trying to impress, she was doing a very good job. I got in as the window closed and I pulled the door shut. The seats were super soft. The leather really did run smooth on the passenger seat. Eleanor was showing her class, she was a rich young blonde bombshell who only had to ask Daddy for anything she desired and behold, it would appear. Bank of Dad was used to the max and this also included a nice top of the range Mercedes and a beauty salon business. Her perfume was all over the car as I allowed myself to bathe in its sweet intoxicating fragrance. I studied her whilst she was driving, She was certainly dressed to kill. She could be with any man she wanted and she happened to be with me. Was she mad or was I selling myself short again? I must have something because this is now the second time I have pulled. I began to notice her driving was a little haphazard. She was one of those drivers that drove, but you would never have the sense that they were in complete control. In some instances, it was very unnerving, but I put my trust in the heavens and resigned myself to fate. With a couple of near misses and a few middle fingers, we made it to our destination unscathed.

The restaurant was very upmarket and I felt a little overwhelmed, whereas Eleanor seemed to be in her element. We were guided through a city of tables to a quieter more congenial spot next to a large fish tank, which was a little more private. We sat and I looked around. It wasn't too busy with just under half the tables occupied. Everything here cried opulence and good living. Was Eleanor trying to dazzle me with her fast car, status, and fine dining? Who knows, I was very impressed, I had never been to a restaurant like this before and definitely never had anyone drive me around in a Mercedes. She was working her magic again and how the hell could say no to her. If you put your head in the noose, don't be surprised if it pulls tight around your neck. I started looking at the menu and the prices were out of this world. I had one of those dread feelings, that I really didn't like as they often signal impending doom. I was in an awkward situation with my incredible shrinking fiver only able to cover a starter. Boy, did I get that wrong? I could get plenty down the local burger bar, but we were far from logic and sensible pricing. My embarrassment started to spill out onto my face.

"Don't worry it's my treat," Eleanor said.

"Are you sure?" I said with relief.

She gave a reassuring smile as she looked again at the menu. Did she sense the anguish and humiliation in my dark moment? From this moment on she would own me and she had bought me for the price of a meal, albeit an expensive one. I would be obligated to pay her back. I would be the gimp in the tight leather outfit, a plaything for her personal amusement and sexual pleasure purposes, to do whatever she commands. Or maybe we could come to some other arrangement which didn't involve the use of my body. I focused on the menu again, I wasn't even that hungry. Eventually, we ordered and were left alone with the tropical fish. Despite being made to feel inadequate I realised that I should try to enjoy the time. The fish were very inquisitive, coming right up to the glass and looking in on our strange world. I put my finger against the glass and moved it slowly around. They followed my finger as if it were a tasty nibble just out of reach with their mouths opening and closing.

"That's really funny," Eleanor said.

"I think they like me," I said.

"Yes, you've made some new friends already," Eleanor said laughing.

"Well, I try to be friendly," I said.

Fish are more intelligent than they appear. Studies have shown that their cognitive powers match or exceed those of non-human primates. They are probably far more intelligent than some people I know, no slight intended. They can even recognise human faces with high accuracy, give responses and memorise. Clearly, they are clever buggers.

It looked like the fish would be our guests for dinner and be a part of our evening. They were very colourful with beautiful markings and the playful side of me was attracted to them as they were to me. I was back to my happy self again as the waitress arrived with the food. Eleanor had ordered more than a few dishes to pick and choose from. These were placed in the middle of the table. I had already eaten, but the food did look delicious, so I indulged in a few selected helpings plus some of Eleanor's recommendations. But mostly, I was watching Eleanor as she tucked in and shovelled her food away. Where was she putting it all? She was such a slim pretty thing and yet she had an appetite of a hungry hippo. The two puppies would surely need feeding and would account for a large percentage of her intake. But I swear, even the fish were wide-eyed and mesmerised. I sipped on the sweet white wine and it was like liquid honey. It was so smooth, I could easily drink it all night. I was still a drinking novice and had already drunk more in the last 24 hours than I had in the whole of my life. I was vulnerable to drink and its consequences with a big mistake already made under its influence and probably more to come. I needed to find my limitations and have more control over my actions than I had at present. Eleanor was smiling at me in a way that suggested that I had already had too much. I was fine, wine with food was not so bad and my head was clear. She poured a glass for herself and joined me with a drink.

"The wine is very good," I said.

"I ordered it especially for you," Eleanor said.

"It's appreciated. Thank you," I said.

I began to feel that Eleanor had a hidden agenda even though she had made all the right noises when I spoke of Sarah. I would try to dispel these thoughts and give her the benefit of the doubt. Even though I didn't love Eleanor, I was still very fond of her and if it wasn't for Sarah, well who knows, she just came along at the wrong time. We had got attached to our table and had decided to stay for a few more drinks. The fish were still captivated by our presence and danced for our amusement and attention as we whiled away another hour or so. Her cheeks became flushed and mine were in all likelihood the same. She had not drunk as much as me. I, however, had passed my safe limit and I was now in a twilight zone of revolving doors and singing fish. It was time to leave our colourful aquatic friends with whom I had formed a warm attachment and make our way back. They would not be forgotten.

We arrived back without incident owing to the empty roads and found a place to park before making our way to the hotel entrance. I could see the lobby area was empty as we made our way over. We walked in together through the front doors with the receptionist giving me a very puzzled look indeed, I put my index finger to my lips as if to say keep it to yourself, mum's the word. We managed to keep our composure all the way to the elevator by supporting each other and acting in a calm dignified way. But as soon as the lift doors closed on us, we both burst out laughing and collapsed on the lift floor. Eleanor fell in such a way that her short dress lifted and her venus mound became visible. I did try to ignore it but it was so beautiful, so I looked some more. Eleanor could see me looking and had

133

gone very quiet with the expectation that something was about to happen. The lift doors opened and momentarily broke the spell as we both crawled out on our hands and knees and made tracks for Eleanor's door. We were void of feline grace and resembled a couple who were mentally challenged in search of that elusive doorknob. After a few false dawns, we made it to her door which was not dissimilar in our sorry states to reaching base camp on Kilimanjaro. We both sat with our backs on her door in a celebratory pause before the long-awaited grand opening. Carefully we managed to get to our feet using the wall to balance and stood precariously at her door. Eleanor opened the door and flicked the light switch as the door closed behind us, we ventured forwards. One step, two steps, over we go again. Once more on the floor, but this time we were going nowhere. It had all been building up to this, from the moment I got in the car, and I had been oblivious to it until now. This was where the silliness would end and our more serious interactions would begin. Eleanor started undoing her blouse and cast it aside to reveal her boulder holders (bra cups). I just had to release her puppies, as I unhooked her clasp they bounced into view. I fondled them and took them for a spin, they were amazing. They defied gravity and stood proudly erect. We moved to the bed as all our clothes randomly hit the floor in our rush for fulfilment. We dispensed with all the preliminaries as we fell onto the bed and moved together. My hands were roaming freely over her soft body feeling her curves, touching her hair and squeezing her bare bum. Her legs were wrapped around me and I was pressing against her love grotto. She was so wet, it just pushed its way in with no assistance, like an uninvited guest who then suddenly became very popular. As I got into my stride there was a knock at the door. We did not answer in our heightened state of pleasure. I mean who the hell would. Excuse me, darling, just let me pull it out at the pinnacle of our gratification and see who is at the door. No, nobody in their right mind would do such a thing, it will never happen. There was a second knock as we were on the final straight. Things were definitely stirring down there as Eleanor started moaning uncontrollably as the noise levels increased. I started looking at her puppies as they bounced to and fro in rhythm with my pushing. You could truly get hypnotised watching them, they were very erotic with large areola around the nipple. As I watched them moving I suddenly felt extremely aroused and it wasn't long before I pushed deep and blew my load. What is this quintessence of lust? I had failed again and yet, I wasn't beating myself up over it. I was weak to women's candy and I would just have to accept it. I would try to be good to Sarah in a bid to make up for my shortcomings. I did love Sarah and without any doubt in my mind, she would be the one I would choose over all others. My attraction to women of all types was a built-in flaw in my character that I would just have to live with. It was time to be rational and realise that I was not perfect, there is good and bad in everyone and I was no different. I returned from my thoughts and relaxed in bed for a while as Eleanor was talking to me about jumping on a train to come and see her. She didn't know that I wasn't free to do as I pleased, at least not yet. Maybe someday we could meet again, but it wouldn't be anytime soon. I didn't want her to be disappointed in me so I took one of her beauty salon cards and gave the impression my visit would be relatively soon. It made her happy and I wasn't ruling out seeing her at some point no matter how slim. It was time to go, as I started to get ready and as I picked up my clothes from the floor, I could see a paper that had been pushed under the door and I went to investigate. Blimey, it was from Bill and he wanted to see me. The note was making me feel uneasy, this was a real shit sandwich and I didn't want to eat it. But then I remembered it was Bill who was my confidant and friend. I respected him and would just have to take whatever he decided, good or bad. If I had to choose anyone in the school to deal with something like this, it would be Bill. My future was now hanging in the balance, but I was philosophical as my whole life up to this point had been a series of pitfalls and recoveries. I would survive in some form or another, besides they needed me to help win the league and our Headmaster really wanted the trophy this year.

"Is everything OK Paul," Eleanor said.

"Yes, It's just my friend Beefy. He's getting lonely," I said.

I didn't want to alarm Eleanor so I lied about the letter in order to protect her, I would fix it without getting her involved. I couldn't see Bill now as it was very late but I'm sure I would receive a visit in the morning and get a chance to explain myself. I'm a bit fragile in the mornings and my confidence takes time to grow, so I would need a good story with good delivery and a lot of luck.

"Do you want to smoke," Eleanor said

"Not now but you can roll me one for later," I said.

I finished getting ready and got comfortable beside her as she passed me a very large rolled joint. Beefy will be ecstatic when he receives his first joint and he will say with great pride that I gave it to him. The trouble is, where the hell will I say that I got it from. Smoke filled the air like a dense fog as Eleanor inhaled and released, I was not smoking but I was still getting a comfortable buzz just by being next to her. I put my head on her breast and started to relax with my thoughts focused on my meeting and how I would deal with all the early questioning. This was no good, I needed a clear head for my morning interrogation with Bill, so I gave Eleanor a kiss with a long warm hug and said goodbye. From my side, the finality of our goodbye was indisputable, if she didn't see me within a few weeks she would move on and I understood that. She was a young woman and her needs would override any dwindling sentiment that she held for me. Life is about experiences and moments, and my time with her would not be forgotten. Our time had passed, but the memory would not fade. For two nights we defied all the odds, broke all the rules and taboos, and we shone so brightly together. We had lived life to the full without fear of any consequences and I would never get into a Mercedes again without thinking about her. No, I would not forget Eleanor or the fish.

Lime Chapter

The morning came around all too soon and the cold light of day was highlighting my fragility and lack of sleep as I rose like a corpse from the grave. I made my way to the bathroom nursing my sore head. I filled the sink and submerged my face in the warm water until I needed some air. I rubbed my eyes and face with a towel and stared at the mirror. Hells bells, why do you feel and look so bad the morning after a good night out? I wetted my hair and combed it. A good hair day but my face was tired and I was no oil painting. I went back to my bed, Beefy and Kirk were still sleeping. I then went over to Beefy and gave him a gentle shake.

"Wake up Beefy, wake up," I said.

"Hey Paul, umm...... Bill was looking for you last night," He said, yawning.

"What did you say to him," I said.

"I just said that you went downstairs," He said.

"That's good, Thanks Beefy, here I've got you something," I said.

In my shirt pocket was the largest joint and still in one piece. Beefy immediately looked alive and full of vim with his eyebrows doing a Mexican wave. I handed the joint over to him as he ran the length of it under his nose with his eyebrows still rolling.

"Wow, I can't wait to get stoned," He said.

"Well you won't be disappointed, it's pretty strong stuff," I said.

Kirk was awake and caught some of our jabber.

"What strong stuff?" He said.

"Who rattled your cage?... well…you'll find out later," Beefy said.

Kirk smiled, I think he was listening all along. There was a good buzz in the room as Beefy strutted off to the bathroom as if he was on a catwalk.

"What are you going to say to Bill," Kirk said

"I don't know, but it needs to be good," I said.

"His last visit here was at 10 pm. You just need a Jackanory (story)," Kirk said.

Just as Kirk finished speaking there was a knock at the door which I answered and low and behold it was Bill.

"Paul, we need to have a talk so if you can meet me in reception in about 10 minutes and we'll have little a chat," Bill said

" OK Bill," I said.

He nodded as if to emphasize my response had been received, turned and clicked off down the corridor. I closed the door and looked at Kirk.

"Shit, that didn't sound too good," I said.

Kirk agreed, which didn't help, was my fragile world about to implode on itself. I had just 10 minutes to get my clothes on and get my arse downstairs. I did it in 5 minutes and made my way to the reception area. Bill was waiting in a quiet area at a small table by a large window. I went over and joined him.

"Hello Paul, take a seat," Bill said.

I pulled the chair out and sat down.

"Now, before you give your account of yesterday I will let you know what I know...You were seen yesterday night returning with a young lady. We don't know where you had been or what happened after. You can now give your version of events," Bill said.

Houston, we have a problem, but in fact, it's a little bit more than a problem. On the scale of things, its a fucking monster of a problem. Oh shit, I'm fucked and my life is over. My story, that I had memorised word for word through the night had just been blown out of the water with no possible use. I was void of ideas and imagination, the game was up. It was time to crawl under a large stone and stay hidden, possibly forever. Then, a glimmer of light, I would just say that I only went out for dinner. The plan was damage limitation and to keep what happened as innocent as possible. I composed myself and began to speak..

"I met this lady on the first night called Jane and we talked for a while. I never mentioned the school or even that I was at school, so she was unaware of that. We agreed to meet for dinner yesterday and we had a meal not too far from here. We then came back, we said goodnight and parted company," I said.

"OK, so you went out without permission and left the hotel," Bill said.

"I can only say yes," I said.

" Paul, I just want you to know that I'm not getting any joy out of this, it's out of my hands and it will have to go to the Headmaster. I will try and help you with a personal report but my hands are tied. I have to report things like this or it's me for the high jump if they ever come to light," Bill said.

"It's OK Bill, I understand," I said.

"Try not to worry too much. In the grand scheme of things, it's not the worst thing that has happened at Outwood Manor. Just enjoy the day today and it will all be sorted out tomorrow," Bill said.

"I'll try. Thanks, Bill," I said.

Two nights of burning the candle at both ends sorted out with a civilised intelligent chat with the second round in the Headmaster's office. God, I loved this life, dealing with articulate, enlightened, educated people. No need to get hot under the collar, just work it all out rationally to a sensible conclusion. Even the use of force (cane, slipper) was delivered without emotion in a matter of fact way. Stiff upper lip and take it on the chin was expected of all those receiving punishments. I wondered if the same detached behaviour was applied by these individuals in the bedroom. Certainly not me, women are far too exciting to be holding back any of my emotions. They are designed to get you stimulated and aroused and for most men, it really works.

I surfaced back at the room in readiness for the day ahead. Today we would visit the Shipwreck and Diving Museum in Arreton in the middle of the island and afterwards return back to the school. Beefy and Kirk were now ready and relaxing on their beds waiting for me.

"How did it go," Beefy said.

"Got to see Headmaster tomorrow," I said.

"So you're OK for today then," Kirk said.

"Yes, Bill said not to worry," I said.

They both congratulated me and with that, we all bounded off for breakfast with good expectations for the day ahead. After breakfast, we were all waiting in reception with our bags for the coach to arrive. I was keeping a low profile as I didn't want Eleanor to see me with the group, but in truth, Eleanor would be too tired. She would not be up at this early hour and I really had nothing to worry about. The coach arrived and we all stowed our bags and boarded in an orderly manner with Bill and Maurice watching over their motley crew. We were not yet in full swing and still had that morning numbness but given the right conditions we were primed and ready to blow. Simon was up to his usual antics again, this time by contorting his face and pressing it against the window. This, however, was not getting much reaction from people we were passing, so he decided to move to phase 2 on a busy town road. He pulled his trousers and underwear down in one hit and pressed his hairy arse and nut sack against the coach window. He was certainly getting noticed now and the reactions of disgust and amusement from pedestrians were making us all cry with laughter. He had hit the jackpot and it was one of the funniest moments of the trip. We were so busy laughing at Simon, that we failed to notice that Maurice had walked up the aisle and caught Simon red-handed with his pants down. Simon was now facing the high jump along with me tomorrow and I had a feeling that it might take a bit of heat off my situation. Headmaster would take a dim view of Simon's lewd behaviour and he would surely face the cane. So as well as making us all howl with laughter, without even knowing it, he had taken much of the pressure off me. I began to feel more optimistic about my future at Outwood Manor, I would likely be saved just on Simon's more serious conduct alone. Simon was now looking sullen and remorseful and was probably contemplating his date with destiny, i.e., Headmaster with a large cane hovering over his extremely sore buttocks. Good luck with that one Simon.

We arrived at the Shipwreck Museum without further incidents. It was a glorious day and my guardian angel was watching over me. I would survive to break the rules again with my carefree and fearless attitude. Despite being caught, Simon was getting a lot of sympathy from our group including Beefy and Kirk, who were patting him on the back and telling him not to worry. I too expressed my solidarity and support although I secretly knew what was in store for him. I didn't want to bring the mood down and tried to keep things upbeat and give him some false hope. It was the antidote that he needed as his face changed back to that look of comic capers.

As we queued at the ticket office we were joined by another party from a girls school of similar age. Suddenly, we were all adjusting our hair and looking over at them and checking them out. We would most likely never see these girls again after today but there is something within us all that just likes to flirt. The art of appreciating someone for being sexually interesting and having those feelings reciprocated really does make you feel alive, even if that is all there is. Everyone likes to be noticed and this, in turn, gives us the confidence to deal with the opposite sex. Most flirting is playful and mostly never goes any further than boosting your self-esteem, but occasionally when the attraction is strong enough, things will happen. I really didn't expect there would be any danger of that today, if there was, it would be crazy mad wild love.

No, these girls were far too shy and reserved to look at you with longing burning eyes, they would die of embarrassment first.

We made our way into the museum as Maurice led the way with Bill trailing at the back of our group. There would be no hanky panky today. As time went on, and we all meandered around the exhibits, the two groups became quite mixed with the opportunity to get close to the girls. Beefy and Kirk wanted to play a game of dare which each one of us would have to do. So, to make things more interesting, I agreed. The first one was easy, which was to touch a girl on the shoulder. We all managed this without difficulty. The next one would be slightly more tricky. This was to squeeze a girl's bum, with the chance of a rebuke or even a slap. I really wanted to do this one, so I went first. We found a quiet spot and happened upon a redhead girl, redheads are known for being fiery and hot-tempered. I thought she looked a bit prudish as my hand went up her skirt and squeezed her cheek softly and then firmly. To my surprise, she turned her head to look at me but did not move away or even question what I was doing. Instead, she carried on looking at the exhibit and making notes. I moved my hand away only after giving the other cheek a little attention, Beefy and Kirk were gobsmacked, unable to comprehend what they had just witnessed. It was Kirk's turn and we found another candidate, his hand went up her skirt, he didn't linger too long and the deed was done mainly by the element of surprise. She looked a little shocked but again nothing was said. Now it was beefy's turn with the weight of expectation resting with his amateur hands. A victim, sorry I meant a young filly, was chosen and the bets were on. Beefy strolled over unnoticed and stood beside her. She was taller and a looker. He looked somewhat unsure as he went for it, his hand travelled up her skirt and squeezed on the prize. As he squeezed on her buttock a loud scream went out and everyone in the room turned to see Beefy with his hand up a skirt. He was so busted. From our safe vantage point, we saw Maurice run over and remove the offending hand which had not been withdrawn as he was still in shock. No explanation was needed as it had been witnessed by everyone in the room, including Bill, Maurice and the two teachers from the girl's school. In the space of a few hours, there were now three defendants up to see the Headmaster on Misery Monday. Two of us didn't even have a defence, apart from maybe temporary insanity. Apologies were made by Bill and Maurice on behalf of Outwood Manor and assurances were given that the punishment would be severe. In a lot of ways, it was actually worse than Simon's antics as it involved another school. Our poor Headmaster would have to make and receive phone calls on the matter, make a full apology and do a bit of grovelling. He would not be happy. Beefy though did have influence as his family were very rich and his younger brother was also at Outwood, so two lots of annual fees. Our beleaguered Headmaster would have to tread carefully and not upset

Beefy's family with this prickly and sensitive problem.
Bill escorted Beefy away, he had no choice, he
couldn't leave Beefy around the girls with his
wandering hands. Bill didn't know it was just a game
of dare, albeit a tad risque. Beefy was a little out of his
comfort zone with his hand on unchartered territory.
He would now be known as someone who is dangerous
around skirt, this could, in theory, enhance his standing
as a player with the girls at Outwood. He may gain
notoriety and change his life for the better or it could
be seen as something more sinister and ugly or he may
be made to feel ashamed. His life was at a fork in the
road which could decide the direction of his future.
Personally, I didn't think it would make any difference.
He will be rich and get everything that he desires, live
the perfect life and nobody will remember today's
indiscretion. The game was up and Beefy was the clear
loser. It was back to reality looking at diving suits and
pieces of eight, in the forlorn hope things would
improve. They did not and after the girl's school

departed the day could not pass quickly enough. After a packed lunch in the museum picnic area, we were eventually on our way back to Outwood. The mood on the coach was placid and calm with many sleeping and others in thought. Occasional restful conversation interrupted the constant reassuring hum of the coach engine. My thoughts now turned to Sarah and finding some time with her in the regimented routine of Outwood Manor. Simon was also on his best behaviour under the watchful gaze of Bill and Maurice in a mostly uneventful and trouble-free trip.

Maroon Chapter

We arrived back at Outwood early Sunday evening after an eventful weekend, at least from my point of view. We all queued for our bags and then made our way back to Robin Dorm to unpack. It was good to be back, it was a school but it was also my home and I couldn't imagine being anywhere else. I had become institutionalised and I could not visualise how boring a normal family home must be. The limitations of a small family home compared with the vast spaces of a large boarding school with all its facilities. Just inside we had Badminton, Snooker, a full-size trampoline, A massive purpose-made Scalextric, 4 tracks wide which folded away from the wall, table tennis table, a large library, TV rooms for each dorm, cupboards full of board games past and present. We wanted for nothing, all our needs were provided for. We also had an on-site Victorian indoor swimming pool with the original changing lockers, this was where I learned to swim with a doggy paddle. Outside we had a large scale fort made from scaffold boards with walkways and towers. Teachers were not allowed to enter and could only go there in an emergency. Archery was also taught at the fort with the straw target erected in front of the large gated entrance. Any arrows wide of the target would just get embedded in the fort walls. Despite being a maverick and not adhering to many of the rules, I did have an affinity with Outwood Manor and I was loyal in a semi-autonomous way. I was part of the fabric of school life and yet not wholly aligned. I would push back against authority if I thought it was wrong or not in my interest. I was a rebel with a fully functioning brain and not a conformist. I would yield to nobody, I would speak out and never acquiesce. The teachers looked upon me as an oddity and certainly not somebody to be pushed around. My days of being a victim were over and my assertiveness was tangible.

It was time to join evening-association and find Sarah, as I entered the main assembly hall where most of the activities took place, I could not see her. Then I saw Gabby and made my way over. She was listening to music and chatting with two other girls at a table.

"Hey Paul, you're back," Gabby said.

"Yes, we survived the weekend," I said.

"You make it sound so bad," Gabby said.

"It wasn't great, I wanted to stay," I said.

I had to be careful when speaking to Gabby because I knew Sarah would ask her what had been said and Gabby being her best friend would tell her everything. She was very loyal to Sarah.

"Aww, you missed Sarah... She's on the phone," Gabby said.

"Of course I did, Thanks Gabby," I said.

There was a public wall phone in the school with a wooden bench underneath it. The staff room was close but was only used in the day when the teachers were present. In the evening the corridor was only used for the phone, it wasn't very well lit either. At this time it would be quiet. As I approached I could hear Sarah's voice and as I got closer she smiled and put her index finger on her lips. She was talking to her mother, so I sat beside her and laid my head in her lap. She stroked my hair like I was an attention-seeking cat and continued talking with mummy. I did want her attention, but having my hair caressed was pretty cool too. In Fact, I was starting to enjoy it, she had magic hands and they were soothing me again. I really had met my match with Sarah and our personalities fitted perfectly. I was behaving myself and I was kinda tired after the weekend trip. I was just happy being in

Sarah's presence with my head in her lap feeling her stroking my hair intimately. When the call finished I felt her long hair brush across my face followed by her lips pushing on mine. I responded by moving and pressing my lips slowly on hers. I think we were both happy to be together again. The telephone bench was a new venue for us but we could not achieve more than what we were doing in such a public place. After a very long kissing session, we held each other tightly.

"So how was your trip?" Sarah said.

"Not very good. I didn't want to go," I said.

"There must have been some good bits?" Sarah said.

"Simon putting his hairy bum against the coach window and getting caught," I said.

"That's funny, you did have some fun then," Sarah said.

She then started fumbling inside her jeans pocket searching for something and after a short delay produced a very small box and thrust it towards me.

"I bought it to keep you safe," Sarah said.

Not knowing what to expect, I opened the box to reveal a silver Saint Christopher pendant with a chain. This touched me in a way that I still can't fully explain. I suddenly became very emotional with tears flowing from my eyes and I couldn't stop them. It was my guilt and also my sorrow, I was unworthy of such a thoughtful and heartfelt gift. She had spent all of her money on me and I really didn't deserve her affection. Sarah held me in her arms and comforted me, I tried very hard to control myself and gain some composure but it was no good. I pictured her in a shop thinking about me and buying my gift and it really hit home how selfish I had been over the last two days. I could learn a lot from Sarah, she was very mature in many ways, but she was also very sensitive and thoughtful. I began to gather myself together and slowly settle down with my tears eventually drying up. I started to feel a little better with the help of Sarah's warmth and comfort.

"I'm sorry, that's the sweetest, nicest thing that has ever happened to me, It's beautiful just like you," I said.

And with that she was all over me, I had shown her that I do have a heart and I can be affected emotionally. She had touched me deeply with her moving gift which had evoked in me a keen sense of regret. I had also bared my softer side, which seemed to appeal to her and I think she empathised with my words also. I could do no wrong for now. As we kissed the 20.30 bell sounded, which was the bell for everyone to return to their dorms. After one last kiss and a long hug, I let Sarah go back first, then after a few more minutes, I made my way back to Robin Dorm.

My tired eyes opened on a bright sunny morning, then I remembered it was Misery Monday, So I closed them again, but closing my eyes would not make any of it go away. I would have to submit myself to the views of others to make judgements on me and my behaviour. I decided as I was getting ready not to think about it, what will be will be. It would not be a firing squad with the famous last request. I would survive this and life would go on. I was calm and relaxed in the face of uncertainty and ready to dance with the devil. After a hearty breakfast and another boring assembly, we were all sitting outside our overworked Headmaster's office awaiting our punishment. Simon and Beefy were looking very worried and with good reason, they had both sat through breakfast as virtual onlookers taking no part in the banquet of the brave. Simon was the first to enter the Headmasters lair with the outcome not really in much doubt. Headmaster let rip with both barrels in a tirade of expletives in a highly charged encounter, Simon was belittled and vilified for disgusting displays to unsuspecting members of the public. After a moment of quiet Screams echoed around the room as the trusty cane struck Simon's buttocks time and again. Simon endured 12 hefty strokes of the cane and when the door swung open, his face was bright red and he was nursing both buttocks.

He did not speak and made his way back to the dorm. Beefy was next and already shell shocked from all the screaming. He entered gingerly and closed the door. Headmaster kept to the booming voice routine and started with "What the hell possessed you to do such a thing." There was a pause and Beefy replied and probably very well as I could not hear it. Then a change of tone and a calmer voice from Headmaster. There was a steady pause And then screams echoed around the room once again. Beefy's reply was not that good as the cane was now slamming against his backside, but after only six strikes the screaming stopped. For some reason, he had cut Beefy a break. He may have realised that he too had wandering hands that wandered all over a Sixth Former (12th Grade), like a pianist tinkling the fine ivories. Beefy emerged shaken but not stirred, but still very sore. He managed a lacklustre thumbs up as he too made for the dorm. I was now the last of the coach trip rule breakers. As my name was called I entered the shadowy world of the Headmasters office.

What pain and what joy these walls have witnessed. I was asked to sit down and make myself comfortable. Then he cleared his throat ready to speak:

"Look, Paul, you are one of the most respected pupils in the school and in a lot of ways a model pupil. You have achieved so much in your time here and I don't want to see you throw it away. You do though, have a tendency to overstep the mark every now and again which puts me in a difficult position. As far as I know, you were just seen with this woman, and you yourself said that it was just a dinner date. Bill has explained your version of events and in the absence of any other facts or evidence, I am willing to accept that no wrongdoing was intended. Bill has also said that you are a well-behaved member of Robin Dorm and he has never had any problems with you. He has also said that you have helped many in your dorm with their problems. However, you did not inform anybody as to where you were going or even ask permission, so the punishment will be, no more trips for this year. I don't see dinner as a reason for punishment. I am being lenient in the hope that you'll mend your ways. and become the star pupil that we all know you are," Headmaster said.

"Thank you, Sir, I will," I said.

And that was that. I came to realise from this point that some people have a God-given right to break rules and get away with it and others will fall as casualties trying. Allowances could and would be made for certain individuals and to my surprise, I was one of those privileged few. I felt empowered having Bill and Headmaster on my team, I disliked pushing the boundaries, but they were in my way too often and they stopped me from being free and alive. I made my way back to the dorm and met Simon, Beefy and Kirk, all the others were in class. We had a little recovery time before we needed to be back. It was something that was introduced after more than a few pupils pissed their pants being caned and some after. So you now get time to change and time for sore bums to be able to sit again before going back to class.

" So, what happened then," Kirk said.

I couldn't say I got no punishment as they would think there was favouritism involved, so I started rubbing my backside. I looked at Beefy.

"I got 6, the same as Beefy, plus no more school trips this year," I said.

"I got 12 and no school trips this year," Simon said.

Simon had his pants down surveying the damage to his arse and I have to say, it was a horror show. You could see the strike lines of the cane all over, one was even on his lower back.

"You need to see Matron, get yourself ready and I'll take you down," I said.

Simon did not even argue as he got himself together delicately. As we arrived at the Sick Ward, Matron was in her office filling some forms.

"I have a casualty for you Matron," I said peering around the door.

"Paul my dear, how are you," Matron said.
Matron got up and suddenly I was smothered with her extremely large bosom which enveloped me totally.

"I'm OK thanks Matron, but I think Simon needs attention," I said.

"OK, let's get him in and take a look," Matron said. I gave them some privacy as Matron examined the horror show on the other side of a curtain. Matron then came out tutting.

"So, this has just happened Paul," Matron said.

"Yes, Matron," I said.

"OK Paul, if you're going back to class, I want you to tell the teacher that Simon will be in the Sick Ward for at least 5 days," Matron said.
I said goodbye to Simon and thanked Matron before leaving. He would be telling his jokes to the walls in the Sick Ward. Solitude is nice but somebody like Simon needs others to feed off and banter with, he may find it difficult to cope. I was hoping that I would not come up in any conversation about Simon arriving at

the Sick Ward. I had put my privileged position on the line by getting involved, but I did feel that I did the right thing.

As the final buzzer for the school day sounded, my mind was consumed with Sarah and how to give her something back. I still had the five pounds that Beefy had given to me and decided to take an unauthorised trip to the local shops. The route was the usual one, through the hole in the fence at the back of the woods, but there was always the danger of being spotted by someone from the school. There was a knick-knack shop not too far from the cinema which had a small jewellery section. I was heading there, with the breeze in my hair and a warm feeling about spending all my money on a very special person. When I arrived, I scanned the shop window, then I spotted a tray of rings, shiny and bright. They all looked very nice, so I went inside for a closer view. As I entered the shop there was a middle-aged lady arranging a display.

"Can I help you, young man," she said, turning around.

"Yes, I'd like to look at the tray of rings in the window," I said.

She brought the tray over, placed it in front of me and opened it up. I gazed upon them and wondered which one Sarah would choose. The shop assistant seemed very inquisitive.

"Is it for a young lady?" She said.

"Yes, it's for my girlfriend, Sarah," I said.

".I know Sarah very well, she was here on Saturday buying a pendant," She said.

I pulled my pendant out from under my shirt.

"This one," I said.

"Yes, wow, so your Paul, I'm Molly by the way," She said.

I was a little uneasy that someone I didn't know knew my name, what else did she know?

"Hello Molly, I'm surprised you know my name," I said.

"Sarah really likes you. She talks about you all the time," She said.

"Well, I guess if you know her, you may know which ring she likes," I said.

"Of course, Sarah loves jewellery and she comes here every week, mostly just to chat. She likes this one," She said.

Molly pulled a ring carefully from the tray, which had a plain band with a small heart on the front. It looked quite modest and probably not one that I would have chosen. Molly then showed me the inscription on the inside of the band which said "Forever Yours."

"How much is it," I said, appreciating it more.

"It's seven pounds, but for you Paul, five is OK," She said smiling.

Fantastic, the ring that she wants for the money that I have. Couldn't have worked out better. Molly had been very fair and she was growing on me already. I paid her up as she placed the ring in a box and wrapped it.

"Here you are dear, she will like that very much," Molly said.

"Thanks, Molly, she deserves something good," I said.

And with that, I was on my way back with a swing in my step and a new acquaintance added to my friend list. When I got back to Outwood it was nearly dinner time, so I waited with Sarah's present. I didn't want to rush it and I wanted it to be very sincere and also casual. She needed rewarding and up till now I had been a selfish shithead, but now it was all going to change. I will be that person that she holds in such high regard and I will be thoughtful, caring and selfless, just as she is.

Shepherd's Pie, more mash and two veg with lashings of gravy was my favourite and it had to be tonight. It was also followed by butterscotch whip garnished with clementines, another favourite. After excessing in both, my belly was like a snare drum ready to belt out a few tunes. Now I could understand how Cool Hand Luke felt after eating fifty eggs for a bet. I caught up with Sarah about an hour after dinner in the most unlikely of places. She was in the fort with Gabby in one of the towers. As I was walking near the football pitch, I heard Sarah call out my name. I made my way to the tower where Gabby was having a crafty fag (cigarette) and Sarah was coughing.

"Are you OK?" I said, looking at Sarah.

"Yes, I just tried a ciggy and I didn't like it," Sarah said.

"Well, at least you know now," I said.

"Yes, I'll stay clear of them from now on," Sarah said.

Gabby offered me a tug and I had to refuse to show solidarity with Sarah. I sat on the floor with them and rested my back against the tower wall. As I did so Sarah laid her head on my lap and got comfortable.

"More good news… Kirk would like to meet up with you Gabby," I said.

"Really, so he likes me then," Gabby said looking at me expectantly.

"Yes, I really think he does," I said. I think he would take anything offered that was in a skirt, he had done well to get Gabby. She let out an excited scream and then hugged Sarah who was also very happy for her. Kirk may soon find an end to all his built-up sexual frustrations.

"Do you want to meet him now," I said looking at Gabby.

"I'm not ready and I've been smoking," Gabby said.

"You look fine, He won't mind, really," I said.

"OK, where will we meet," Gabby said.

"How about the tree of death, you know, the one I fell off," I said.

"Yes, good idea, I'll be there in about 10 minutes," Gabby said.

I gave Sarah a kiss and made my way back to look for Kirk. I kind of felt a little excited for him, I mean, they could be going at each other in 20 minutes and Gabby was a fit girl.

I found Kirk back in the dorm reading a comic.

"I have something much better for you to do than that," I said.

"What's that," Kirk said.

"Gabby wants to meet you and she's waiting at the tree of death," I said.

"Really, I need to fix my hair," Kirk said.

Why is it, whenever a guy is going to meet a girl, they start messing around with their hair (if they have any), like it's some kind of ritual that has to be strictly adhered to.

"OK, try and be quick," I said.

I sat on his bed waiting and then quickly moved to the one next to it. Kirk's bed had a very strong smell of body odour which was stifling and powerful like a billy goat. Hopefully, his days of spanking the monkey were over and his bed may now smell sweeter for it.

"OK, I'm ready, how do I look," Kirk said.

He looked like he needed some encouragement, So I helped him out.

"Knock out, Kirk," I said.

I gave him some more motivation on the way and as we got near the fort, I waved him on.

"Good luck," I said with a thumbs up.

I didn't think he needed any luck. Gabby was gagging for it and she would be the captain of proceedings, things were going to happen one way or another. I had finally paid Gabby back for helping to get me and Sarah together and it felt good. I was proud of myself. I made my way to the castle and Sarah was standing on the rampart.

"What kept you," Sarah said.

"Sounds like an invitation," I said.

"It could be," Sarah said.

I raced into the castle and climbed the ladder onto the ramparts where Sarah was waiting for me to sweep her off her feet. I moved in quickly clutching her around the waist and delivered a true romantic kiss. I was the king of the castle and Kirk was the dirty rascal in the woods. Sarah took my hand and led me to the tower with the latch door. Once inside, my queen removed her knickers and positioned herself as I gratefully plundered her bestowed treasure with my unbending rod of iron. After some extremely red-hot steamy moments, we fell to the floor breathless and panting. When my breathing recovered and my heart stopped pounding I remembered the ring. I pulled the small box from my pocket and revealed it surreptitiously to gain surprise.

"It's for you Sarah for being so special," I said. She opened the box tentatively and then gasped.

"I've wanted this for so long, how did you know," Sarah said.

"I cheated, Molly said you would like it," I said.

"You met my friend Molly?" Sarah said.

"Yes, we got on well, so you like it then?" I said.

"I do, I like it more because you bought it," Sarah said.

"I'm just glad that you like it," I said.
I leaned forward and kissed her on the cheek and as I pulled away, she grabbed me with both hands and landed a big lingering romantic kiss right on the lips.

"Thank's Paul, I'll keep it always," Sarah said.
There was a knock on the door then a short silence.

"Are you there Paul," It was Beefy.

"Yes, what is it Beef," I said.

"Open the door," Beefy said.
We made ourselves descent then I opened the door. Beefy was holding the mother joint and his eyebrows were again doing the Mexican Wave.

"I'm going to smoke it now, so the more the merrier," Beefy said.

"I don't want any," Sarah said.

"No, you don't have to. Will you stay anyway," I said.

"OK, just for you," Sarah said.

Beefy was running the joint under his nose and was probably high already. We all sat on the floor as he struck the match which would ignite the dormant bud. A few puffs and it was glowing and giving off its distinctive aroma. As he took one last puff, there was a knock on the door. We all started wafting the air around us.

"Who is it," I said.

"It's Gabby and Kirk," Gabby said.

I opened the door and the pair of them were grinning like two Cheshire Cats.

"And what have you two been up to," I said knowingly.

"This and that...My God, it smells like a cannabis den," Gabby said.

"Yes, it's all kicking off in here," Beefy said.

Gabby and Kirk sat as the magic bud passed between us like a magic game of pass the parcel with everyone becoming a winner with each tug. Even Sarah who was not in the game was getting a passive high just by being here. The smoke only had two narrow open window holes to escape from and it was hanging in the small room. The tower room would smell for days after, if not weeks. Good job the teachers were not allowed in the fort. The joint rapidly diminished in size and our inhibitions fell like crumbling walls, we were talking nonsense and Sarah was not looking happy.

"I'm going back, There's more smoke in here than a kippers smokehouse," Sarah said.

"I'll join you," I said.

I was feeling a little dizzy as we both made our way onto the ramparts and filled our lungs with the fresh evening air. It was great, fresh air is underrated.

"I'm sorry, I know it's not really your thing," I said.

"Your damn right it isn't," Sarah said.

Were we having an argument, I wasn't sure, but it wasn't from my side. Maybe she had seen a side of me that she didn't like or she felt left out and sidelined. I just wanted Beefy to enjoy his first joint with his friends. I suddenly became aware of why she was so upset. Our time together had been going so well before it was interrupted and she had all my attention until Beefy knocked on the door.

"Come here," I said.

"No, I'm annoyed," Sarah said.

"Please, I know why you're upset...Come here," I said.

She came towards me reluctantly and stood in front of me in the twilight. She looked angry and guarded. I stepped forward and put my arms around her as she slowly melted in my loving embrace with all her fiery resistance dissolving away.

"I'm sorry that we didn't have more time and I should have shown you more attention," I said

"Sorry I got moody," Sarah said.

The evening bell sounded as we were still hugging and it was time to part.

"So we're OK now," I said.

"Yes," Sarah said smiling.

I walked her to the main door and she blew me a kiss as she went inside. The more I got to know Sarah, The more I liked her. She had a fragility and there was definitely something in me that wanted to protect and shield her.

Blue Chapter

A couple of days later it was the weekend and for those of us still around, there would be a local trip to a large park not too far away, which was a regular place that we visited. I was not banned from local trips, so I was good to go. The Park Rangers were always on high alert whenever we were around as our capers generally involved a loose interpretation of the park rules. The boating lake was a big favourite and rowing the boats into each other at speed was also very popular, especially when an opposing boat capsized. If someone was liked they would be rescued, if they weren't, they would be pushed away with the oars and made to swim to the bank. Many of us would return to the school dripping and sodden from our battles with each other and also by trying to escape from the Park Rangers. There was an island on one side of the lake which was adjacent to the main bank pathway and was off-limits with signs saying "No Trespassing" everywhere. The small island had been populated with large painted stone dinosaurs and anyone walking the bank pathway would gaze up at these magnificent stone beasts. The dinosaurs were made well but with limited anatomical knowledge and far from what we know they look like today. Creative liberties had been taken and what they didn't know back then, they just made up, with no fear of any contradiction. A visit to the island was something we always did, sometimes we were chased and sometimes we were left alone depending on who was on duty. Once on the island, each standing dinosaur had an open service hole underneath. You could literally climb up into the large cavernous belly of the beast, which would comfortably host six scallywags for a smoking party. From the outside, they had smooth detailed contours and masses of mortar and brick must have been used to achieve the overall result. The inside was a brick construction with some scaffolding (scaffolding was probably added later). There were two large holes, one in the underbelly and one in the mouth. From the mouth, you had a good view of the opposite bank and pathway with at least 180 degrees field of vision. We would wait for onlookers to walk by and blow large plumes of smoke out of the beast's mouth and sometimes large crowds would gather to watch this curious event. Inevitably, it would lead to the Park Rangers coming onto the island looking for the instigators and then a chase would ensue. We would never give ourselves up easily and the thrill of the chase was just that, an adrenaline rush of evading capture. They would unwittingly enter our game, where our motto was,

"Escape at all costs." We would even swim across the lake rather than face getting caught by the Rangers. Anybody who did get caught was sworn to silence and would surely face the wrath of the Headmaster on their return. I don't know why we became so wayward and rowdy, it was like pack mentality with added peer pressure. I think we did it also to break up the repetitiveness of daily life and to do something by your own actions is to truly feel free. The constraint of relentless rules and conformity day after day in a school institution can be soul-destroying, having said that, whenever I was away, I would miss it, go figure. If the Park Rangers had any vestige of sense, they could have just waited by the school bus for us all to turn up one by one, this never happened. Maybe they enjoyed the thrill of the chase as much as we did.

On our return to Outwood, I decided to visit Simon in the Sick Ward. We had not heard from him since he was admitted on the day of his cane injuries. He would surely be going out of his mind by now with only the walls for company. Possibly, Matron was giving him some extra attention, bedside chats and tucking him up in bed. She would be sympathetic and probably feeding him biscuits and milk every day on top of the school meals. I have fond memories of my time there and Matron was the talisman that made everything good. I arrived at the Sick Ward straight from the trip and luckily I was still dry. Matron was in her small office just off the ward.

"Hello Matron, I've come to see Simon," I said.

"Paul my dear, how are you," Matron said. Matron was always so happy and had the ability to cheer up anyone instantly. She got up, opened her arms and pulled me into her large bosom. I was cocooned on all sides by her warm heaving bust and then released to draw air again.

"Come, I'll take you over to Simon," Matron said. She walked me to the end of the ward where Simon was watching TV and laying on the couch with his feet up.

"I'll bring you both some milk and biscuits," Matron said.

"Thanks, Matron," I said.

"Hey Simon, how are you?" I said.
I patted him on the shoulder as he made room for me on the sofa. He was looking very well and his time on the ward had been good for him.

"Matron has been really good, I didn't know she was so nice," Simon said.

"Yes, she looked after me well when I was here," I said.

"You know she had an argument with Headmaster over my injuries. She said if it happens again that she'll be reporting him," Simon said.

"Really!" I said.

"Yes, it happened right here in the ward. He came to see why I was in here and she gave him a few home truths and sent him packing with his tail between his legs," Simon said.

"Wow, I would have paid good money to see that," I said.

Right on cue, Matron arrived with the milk and biscuits on a tray and set it on the coffee table.

"There you are my dears, eat up and drink up," Matron said.

"And how is Sarah young Paul," Matron said.

"She's the loveliest, nicest person I know," I said. It just came out without even thinking about it and this was in front of Simon who probably thought I had gone soft in the head but I didn't care. I gave Simon a rye smile as if to say, you have now seen another side of me.

"That's really sweet Paul, your right, she is and you need to take care of her," Matron said. Matron was so intuitive and always seemed to have her finger on the pulse of what was happening in the school. Matron's grapevine seemed to have no rivals, in my case, it was spot on. She was in the background and always on the side of the pupils, rather than the teaching faculty. We were her flock and she watched over us. She rubbed my head playfully and then went back to her small office. She was great.

"Milk and biscuits ay! I bet you've been having this every day," I said.

"Most days, I didn't think I would like it at first, but I have and it's my last night tonight, so it's kind of sad," Simon said.

"I know what you mean, I missed it too," I said. We finished all the Bourbons, Custard Creams, Jammy Dodgers And Orange Creams with just the plain biscuits remaining, which was good, because Matron liked the plain ones with her tea.

"Well it's been good seeing you Simon, I will let everyone know that you're back tomorrow," I said.

"Thanks for coming Paul," Simon said. I gave him a pat on the shoulder and a wink as I left him to enjoy his last night in the Sick Ward. I also thanked Matron on the way out and she made a point of telling me to visit more often. She made you feel wanted and it wasn't just me, it was everyone. She was a very likeable lady.

On Sunday morning after breakfast, we were given the news that Shirley Green had lost their last game on Saturday, so without even kicking a ball, we were crowned champions. Our triumphant Headmaster was beyond himself with happiness, after 7 years of disappointment, near misses and heartache the Surrey Schools Trophy was finally his to polish to a high shine and admire. The buzz of excitement was filtering through the school and spirits were high. A special school assembly would now be held on Monday where our winner's medals would be presented and the cup displayed for all to see. Halcyon days indeed, but from this amazing high, a fall of spectacular proportions would occur and the source would forever remain a mystery. Word had got out that I dated an older woman on the school trip and it was spreading like wildfire. Students that I didn't even know were congratulating me. I lost count of all the handshakes, shoulder rubs, fist bumps that had transpired. To them, I was a hero, the gigolo student that gave them hope of bountiful female treasures, but for me, my world was falling down around me. I would definitely not be able to talk my way out of this one, there would be no recovery and Sarah would hate me forever. I was already conscious that things were now out of my control and the indignation of the young woman that I loved was my only concern. I resolved to find her and plead to her sensible side, but she was nowhere to be found. Eventually, I found Gabby.

"Hey Gabby, do you know where Sarah is," I said.

"I told Sarah I wouldn't speak to you," Gabby said. She was kind of dismissive of me and acted like she had things to do.

"Listen, I really need your help Gabby, I've hated myself ever since this happened and if I could take it back I would," I said.

"Have you got any idea how upset she is? she's been crying in bed and I don't think she will be down today," Gabby said.

"I'm so sorry, I would never want to hurt her," I said.

"I don't think she wants to see you anymore," Gabby said.

"I'm not going to give up on Sarah, I made a big mistake and I regret it totally. I still love Sarah," I said.

"Paul I have to go, I don't know what she would say to any of that," Gabby said.

Gabby left, but at least I now knew that Sarah did know, even though it had not gone down very well. I was now in the nightmare of the Tree of Knowledge dream and in that scenario, I ended up killing myself. I waited for Sarah to come down all day, Gabby was right, she did not show anywhere. I was going out of my mind with torment and not being able to speak to her was making it worse. You could say that I deserved this and you would probably be right, but who in life has not made foolish mistakes that they regret, I would say not many. Tomorrow would be a day of celebration for all, and Sarah would have to show up unless she was sick. I did not hold out much hope that things would change, but I would have to try and try I would.

It was the day of the presentation assembly and I did see Sarah at breakfast, although she made no eye contact with me. Our triumphant Headmaster wanted us to wear our football kits for the medal awards and have a few pictures holding the cup. This should have been a great day in my life, but all I could do was think about my problems with Sarah. At the assembly, we all took positions standing in line behind our exuberant Headmaster who was on the podium, behind a lectern, looking down on the masses. He made a long speech on the trials and tribulations of football and getting to this point of receiving a nice shiny cup. He had endured a very long wait and his excitement was positively infectious. I was trying to make eye contact with Sarah but she wasn't playing. When we started to receive our medals she was clapping when they were awarded, but when it came to my turn, she did not clap and she looked at me coldly. If looks could kill, I would be dead. It was like a knife in my heart and it was very hurtful, she was obviously in no mood to be nice and I had got the message. This was the worst possible outcome and I was hurting badly. I just wanted things back the way they were, but that now seemed an impossibility. We posed with our medals and took turns holding the cup as the cameraman clicked away. Everyone was enjoying this moment apart from me, I was just going through the motions with my smile masking my sadness and waiting for it all to be over.

The summer was all but finished and a bleak cold winter lay ahead without the warmth of Sarah's love. I had kicked myself so many times over my stupidness, but it would not change a thing. I had approached Sarah frequently over the last month to try and fix

things, Time and time again, I was repeatedly
dismissed as the guy who lies and cheats. The trust had
gone and without it there was nothing. I had lost my
sparkle and became more solitary and remote, my
spectacular rise to the top would be accompanied by a
deep descent to the bottom. Sure there were other girls,
but that would have just added more fuel to the fire and
I didn't want a substitute. I was in the wrong and I only
wanted Sarah. Two more weeks passed with all my
attempts to have a constructive conversation with her
failing, she was showing no signs of weakening and
my hopes were fading. I didn't care about my
reputation anymore, the only thing that meant anything
to me was Sarah. I would have to lay it all on the line
and bare my soul to convince her that I was serious. It
would be the hardest thing that I have ever had to do
and the courage required would be great, with no
certainty of a good outcome. I searched for her and
found her in a close to full classroom, where the
teacher had not arrived yet. They were all standing

around and sitting on tables. It was not my class and there were a few giggles as I approached Sarah. She looked a little shocked that I had gone to this length but at least she was not angry. Perhaps she didn't want to make a scene in front of so many classmates. I stood in front of her and took a deep breath.

"What do you want Paul, you have two minutes," She said.

This was the first time she had given me two minutes, maybe she wanted everyone to see how desperate I was. I composed myself, as I tried to shut everyone else out and focus on Sarah.

"I want you to know that I am far from perfect in many ways, I am trying to fix that. What I do know is that I care for you very much and you are always in my thoughts. Life without you has been hell and I realize how much I miss you. You are the love of my life and nobody can replace you. What I can't do is take all this hatred that you're giving me, I am being destroyed day by day. If you still cared even a little, I could cope...I love you, Sarah, I know that now and whatever happens, at least I have told you," I became distraught. Words had deserted me and my emotion was overflowing with grief for the love I had lost. The torment had been too much for me to handle and it had overwhelmed me completely. I was utterly alone and abandoned as the realisation began to bite. I broke down in front of her, and as I knelt there sobbing at her feet, I felt her hand softly touch my head and then slowly stroke my hair back, she knelt down with me and as I looked up through my tear-soaked eyes, she embraced me tightly and love flowed between us again. The class then proclaimed their sympathy with congratulatory claps and whistles. I held her in my arms not wanting to let go. We were united in love and not ashamed to show it. Our enduring bond had overcome an insurmountable problem and I was so sincerely grateful to have her back. I wished I could hold her forever, I wished and I wished again, but most of all I wished to be the man she deserves and to make her happy.

Printed in Poland
by Amazon Fulfillment
Poland Sp. z o.o., Wrocław

62558840R00122